Lifetime Benefits

A novel by

Don J. Kappel

Major, U.S. Marine Corps (Ret.)

Author's Acknowledgement

Special thanks are due to Joan M. Kappel and our daughters, Courtney and Brooke, for their never-ending love and encouragement as this novel took form over several years, from concept to completion. They were the fuel that kept the work alive.

For her part, Joan took the journey with me for 13 of the 22 years I spent as a Marine, and actual parts of that military career, as well as my follow-on career in Virginia local government, provided experiences that served as impetus for story ideas woven into the background of this novel.

Along the way, many others, from other family members to co-workers, neighbors and friends, expressed their own eagerness to read *Lifetime Benefits*.

With much appreciation, I humbly thank them all and hope they enjoy the book.

— Don J. Kappel

CONTENTS

C H A P T E R 1

Richmond, Virginia

Mike DePalma was surprised…and angry. He was half-heartedly watching the news but turned down the volume on the television and shifted his feet from the sofa to the coffee table. The Scotch whisky was mostly ice now, but still with enough taste to make it worthwhile sipping. Pasta sauce was simmering gently on the stove in the kitchen, but he wasn't hungry yet and it was okay for now.

A stack of papers on the table continued to torment him. His anger was directed at the universe—not at God; because he had been raised to believe that His plans were just things we could never hope to understand. But this was one of those times in life that caused him to seethe with the frustration of not being able to change something that seemed so wrong.

As an Archer Global Life Insurance Company agent, Mike kept busy. He had clients all over Virginia and the Mid-Atlantic area, and also some others he'd signed who had since moved and now lived as far away as San Diego, Houston and Ft. Lauderdale. His Richmond, Virginia, corporate office was a big one, and he was one of the top sellers already, even as one of the relatively newer agents hired.

***

"I can't believe I have to process three policies before Monday. This has been a rough couple of days," he thought. He had half expected one, maybe even two of the deaths to occur sometime in the next year. When you sell life insurance, you do so with the knowledge that eventually, some of your clients' families are going to collect on it.

MaryAnn Trumbull was 91 and the pneumonia had hit her hard. Her son had called him last week to be sure the policy was still in effect, and to ask how he could access the money "if and when" his mom succumbed. The family hated the thought of losing her, but it was clear to everyone that she was deteriorating and had little strength left to fight. She'd languished for nearly two weeks, but lately, it wasn't looking good. Mike had visited with her at Virginia Commonwealth University Medical Center--VCU for short--where she was hospitalized.

When she did pass, he was glad to be able to help the family pay for her funeral expenses and have enough left over to help with some of the great-grandkids' future college expenses, which MaryAnn had told him was one of her wishes. It was one of the things he liked about his new career—helping people with whom he'd established a relationship ensure that their wishes would be brought to fruition when they passed.

Even Bill Wilford, with whom he'd gotten to be very familiar since signing him, was an understandable casualty. He had worked hard, and drank hard, all his 64 years -- and it showed. He had numerous ailments—arthritis, gout, high blood pressure and those kinds of things, but it was his liver that had paid the highest price for his past sins. He was a hell of a good plumber, though. Mike had called on him once or twice over the past year as faucet leaks and running toilets needed attention.

Mike wasn't totally clueless about home repairs, but they weren't his favorite things to do, and even though he could have made the repairs himself, he knew Bill always could use a few bucks. Besides, he got things fixed fairly quickly, and done right the first time. Mike also enjoyed talking with Bill, who often shared advice about the best bars and breweries in the area. It seemed as though he knew them all, and Mike was sure a lot of places that sold alcoholic beverages would be missing Bill's visits.

It was Marvin Kincaid's death that shocked and upset him the most. Marv's wife, Cathy, called Mike to say that her husband had passed away unexpectedly in the early morning hours on Thursday. Marvin was only 39 and seemed active and healthy when Mike had seen him less than a month ago. Marv, as he preferred to be called, had contacted Mike and said he wanted to increase his life-insurance coverage, and Mike stopped by his house to have him sign a couple of documents.

Marv was an Army veteran, having enlisted right out of high school. After a mostly uneventful military career, he had served in Iraq during Desert Storm. He'd been with an infantry unit and saw action in a firefight with Saddam Hussein's Republican Guard units, just about the only Iraqi military component that could shoot straight.

In what military folks call "zigging when he should have zagged," he was hit by small arms fire, but the Army patched him up, gave him a Purple Heart medal and allowed him to finish out his enlistment and retire with 20 years of service.

Now, without ever seeing 40, he left a wife and three young boys. Andrew, 14, resembled Cathy. Nicholas, 11, seemed to look most like Marvin's father, and was already nearly as tall as his older brother. Jason, the youngest at 8, looked so much like his dad that everyone said he was Marvin's clone.

The two younger boys were running around the room, playing, when Mike had visited to do the paperwork, and Marv had invited him out onto the screened porch to get away from the racket.

As a Marine Corps veteran, Mike had served with Army, Air Force and Navy units at one time or another. He even worked with the Coast Guard at Guantanamo Bay, Cuba, for a couple of months on a humanitarian mission to help Haitian refugees. He had not known much about the "Coasties" before then, but had found them to be professional and very dedicated.

All of the military branches were good at what they did, but he was a Marine through and through—hard-charging and someone who exemplified the old axiom, "Once a Marine, always a Marine." Even now, he exercised regularly to keep his five foot, eight inch frame lean and strong. He was patriotic and appreciative of his country and never failed to swell with pride whenever the American flag marched by. Unquestionably, he respected all those who served in the other branches as well. He wished the NFL did. He was so disgusted with football players kneeling during the National Anthem that he hadn't watched a single NFL game since all that crap started.

As veterans, he and Marv had hit it off quickly and their relationship transcended the normal insurance business arrangement. They teased each other about the relative virtues of the Army and the Marines.

They joked about which was tougher and spoke of historic battles. Mike had suggested that maybe; just maybe, General George Patton might have qualified to be a Marine. He also expressed the opinion that Rambo, too, had a slight chance of being tough enough to be a Marine...maybe. That got a laugh out of Marv.

"Yeah, you Army guys are pretty tough," Mike had said, "but Marines are harder than woodpecker lips." That always got Marv to laugh even more. Their inter-service rivalry, as it was for most in the military, was good-natured.

They had become buddies. Marv's wife even tried to fix Mike up with girls a few times. Mike liked to toss a football around with Marv and his boys when he could. It was a nice family and he was glad to be their insurance agent and their friend.

He knew that Marv took several prescription drugs. It was his job to know about his clients' medical history prior to issuance of their life insurance policies. In fact, a physical exam and complete medical records were prerequisites in order to have a life insurance policy issued by Archer Global Life.

Marv's file indicated that he had atrial fibrillation, but it was treated with prescription medications and a letter from his primary care physician stated that it was under control. Marv was athletic and muscular, did all the yard work and other household maintenance and enjoyed working on Cathy's car and his pickup truck.

Except for his slightly longer hair, Marv could have passed for an active duty soldier. Mike didn't know of anything that should have been a serious-enough medical condition to lead to Marv's premature death at such a young age.

Now, he wondered if Marv had a premonition, or if he perhaps just had not been feeling well, resulting in his decision to increase his life insurance coverage. In any event, the processing had been finalized a couple of weeks ago, and Cathy and the children would benefit from the additional money they'd now receive.

While he was deep in thought about Marv, the timer on the stove jarred him. The linguine was bubbling away and now al dente, just the way he liked it. He'd made the sauce the way his mom did, in a big, cast iron frying pan. Some garlic, onion, oregano and olive oil had been the start, with a large can of tomatoes and some salt and pepper rounding out the flavors. He preferred it to the jarred stuff, and it was easy enough to make. Right about now, it smelled terrific.

He turned off the television, uncorked a bottle of Chianti and twirled the pasta slowly, knowing that when he was done with dinner and a planned cigar, he had at least an hour of paperwork to do so he could go to the office Monday thoroughly prepared. Worse still, he had to go to three funerals soon. He always tried to go when a client died. Nobody really expected an insurance agent to do that, but he did get involved with the clients and their families, and wanted to show respect.

Dinner finished, he put the dishes in the dishwasher and stepped out on his small balcony. An old, beat up commercial box truck moved slowly across the bumpy cobblestone street in front of his building, clacking along on its way to or from a delivery, no doubt. He slid into one of the two black plastic Adirondack chairs and lit up a cigar.

This one was a Romeo Y Julieta, a Dominican robusto that was one of his regulars. Rolling the cigar gently in his fingers as the flame from his disposable lighter turned the tip red and then white-gray as ash formed, he puffed, sighed and settled into the chair for what would be a relaxing 20 minutes of escape from the stress prior to hitting the paperwork. The cigar was mild and he enjoyed the easy draw.

Only a few cars crept down the cobblestone street below at this hour of the night, their headlights refracted wildly by the century-old stones. He enjoyed living in the Shockoe Slip area of downtown Richmond. It offered some nice loft apartments, eclectic shopping and excellent restaurants. It also was adjacent to Interstate 95 and not far from I-64. Those two highways took you just about anywhere you needed to go...North, South, East or West.

In fact, from Richmond, Mike could be in Washington, D.C.; Raleigh, North Carolina; Virginia Beach or the mountains to the west, all in less than 2 and a half hours.

Snuffing out the last inch of the stogie, he went inside and spread his copy of Marvin Kincaid's policy, along with Bill's and MaryAnn's, on the kitchen table and made sure he had everything in order. He had to attach a myriad of medical forms and background paperwork to each deceased client's file.

It took a while, but finally satisfied that he had it all put together as needed, at least insofar as a couple of missing documents for Marvin allowed, he put everything into his portfolio, exhaled slowly, and set it all aside.

C H A P T E R

2

Ghost

He awoke early on Monday morning upstairs in his loft bedroom overlooking the street and headed downstairs to grab some coffee, scan his iPhone and check for any significant world news and the weather forecast from the local NBC affiliate. Then he showered, dressed and fired up the old, white Mercedes in the public parking garage around the corner, just past the venerable, landmark Tobacco Company restaurant.

The restaurant was unique for its four floors and history as a former tobacco warehouse back in the 1860s. Inside, diners could still see original brickwork and beams. The menu was extensive, and the prime rib was about the best Mike had tasted anywhere. He didn't eat there often, but he liked having it right near his apartment and parking garage. Sometimes after a long week, he enjoyed a draft beer in the downstairs bar.

Mike had a habit of naming his cars. The first one, a used, blue Volkswagen beetle he bought when he started college, he'd called "Max." He really liked that one. He smiled as he remembered the day he bought it. He told the salesman that he didn't know how to drive a stick shift. The salesman told him he could teach him in about 15 minutes. So, he practiced in the dealership's parking lot and then drove home, only bucking or stalling once or twice. After that, it was a cinch.

Since then, he had owned half a dozen cars or so, mostly old heaps he bought when he was still young and didn't have much to spend. Later, his time in the Marines, with anticipated duty station transfers every now and then, made buying an expensive new car seem like a bad idea.

Not only that, but the enlisted troops tended to have the new cars. They lived in the barracks, ate in the Mess Hall and got their uniforms provided, so they often had more ready cash than the junior officers like Mike did, especially the young married officers.

Now that he was out of the Marine Corps, he finally was able to buy a clean, used, luxury car. He had named the white Mercedes, "Ghost." He'd bought it from the Richmond-based used car market, CarMax, and even though it had quite a few miles on it, it was in great condition and was very fast. He liked opening up the big 8-cylinder engine now and then when he was on some back road with a nice straight section and no cops around. Ghost was a bad-ass!

But today, there was the normal city traffic as he drove through his neighborhood and then eased onto Interstate 95. He lived about 20 minutes from the office, and generally didn't mind the drive, which gave him time to think and plan his day while listening to talk radio—WRVA usually—or the jazz CDs he favored. For contemporary programming, Q-94 FM was usually pretty good, too. For this trip, it was Chris Botti's "Boston" CD. Botti was smooth, and he found his music really relaxing. Ghost had good speakers, too.

I-95 here in Richmond was much like it was all along the eastern U.S. In the urban corridor, it was flanked on both sides by commercial trucking and RV sales lots, parking lots, ball fields, cell towers and old factories. High voltage power lines stretched across the landscape like massive spider webs, seeming to interconnect the cheap motels.

Billboards offered attorneys' services; advertising opportunities; Emergency Room wait times, motel rates and even salvation. Today there was one billboard he liked. "Marines Fight To Win," it read. "Damned straight!" he thought.

As he merged onto I-95, he passed by the historic 1901 Richmond Main Street Station, its Beaux-Arts architectural style a distinctive part of the city's skyline, viewed by millions of passing motorists each year. Across I-95, VCU Medical Center, flanked by its huge, multi-level garage, was joined by the Bank of America and Wells Fargo buildings as among the tallest in the area.

Heading north, he soon saw The Diamond, Richmond's hulking old baseball stadium, its bright array of exterior colors belying its interior condition. He'd been to a couple of Flying Squirrels games and hoped they'd finally decide what to do about either modernizing the stadium or building a new one.

It was one of those ongoing topics in Richmond that never seemed to get solved, like the perennial turmoil over which monuments to build, relocate or remove completely. Parochial interests, Civil War history, various peoples' pride and egos always seemed to get in the way of solutions in Richmond and the surrounding counties. Then again, that kind of controversy was going on in other states lately, too.

———·:·———

As if taking down a monument can change history, Mike thought. *America has come a long way. Those monuments mark times when we were not as enlightened as we are now, nor as dedicated to equality. The times were different and the world simply had not evolved to the point where it had today in terms of how all the different races, religions and cultures got along.*

As for the monuments, he thought they served a valuable teaching purpose right where they are... but not everyone felt that way. For some, they were painful reminders of a past that was cruel. He could see it from both perspectives. But, he thought the monuments should stay put, maybe with others or some context added.

Still, just recently, Richmond City Schools had decided to name a school for the former president of the United States. Mike couldn't help but wonder, since the guy was so unpopular with half the nation, whether someday, that school would end up being renamed again. To him, schools just should not be named for anyone anymore. It always led to somebody being upset. One person's hero is another's villain, he realized.

In the diminishing rural sections, the omnipresent Virginia pines loomed tall and thick, much as they had hundreds of years ago when Pocahontas and British settler John Rolfe were getting to know each other pretty well down south a bit in what is now nearby Chesterfield County. Today, it's a popular tourist spot. Back then it was the 1611 Citie of Henricus.

———·:·———

Whether they actually were married there or elsewhere in Virginia is still debated by historians, but they lived there, and the site is picturesque. Mike had driven out to Henricus once and thought it was interesting from the perspective of American history, but even more so from a military point of view.

The early English settlers had built the settlement high on a bluff overlooking the James River. Stockade fences on one side protected them from the Native Americans when relationships soured and the river and sheer cliff walls would help to protect them from the Spaniards, if they ever came... which they didn't.

As with the monuments, those decisions probably seemed to make sense at the time, even though today, those fortifications would not offer any protection at all.

Of special interest to Mike as a Marine, Henricus and the nearby other bluffs overlooking the river held a unique place in the history of the U.S. Marine Corps. On May 15, 1862, the U.S. Navy vessel, USS Galena, sailed up the James River near there as part of a Union force intending to reach the capital of the Confederacy in Richmond.

Confederate forces had blockaded the river at a bend near Fort Darling, which overlooked the river at Drewry's Bluff. They had planted mines, sunk some boats and added other obstacles in the river. Heavy volumes of small arms fire and cannon blasts forced the Union ships to turn back.

During the intense battle, most of the Navy gunners on the Galena were killed. Corporal John Mackie, a New York native who had enlisted into the 86-year-old U.S. Marine Corps on April 24, 1861, rallied some other Marines and sailors and helped the Galena continue to return fire from the ship's cannons onto the Confederates on the bluff.

For his bravery under fire and leadership of his Marines, Mackie was awarded the nation's highest military award for valor, the Medal of Honor. Many Marines would follow over the proud history of the Corps, many posthumously, but Corporal John Mackie would forever hold the distinction as the first.

Chesterfield County, neighboring Henrico County and the Henricus Foundation had done a good job building a reconstruction of the Henricus village, based on historical documents and archaeological remains.

Reflecting on that time, and thinking tactically as a Marine about the challenges of defending against the local Native American tribes and the Spaniards with the simple muskets of that time, before he knew it, he reached his exit and nosed Ghost into a parking space.

3

Archer Global

Archer Global's offices were just around the corner. The building was tucked behind a smaller one and down a wide alley accented by a large, wrought-iron gate that was open now. Forgoing the elevator, he entered the lobby and ran briskly up the stairs to the second floor, then down the hall to the cluster of offices where he worked. It never failed...every time he took the stairs instead of an elevator, he thought back to his Marine Corps days, where taking an elevator was scorned as a cop-out and somehow "not Marine-like." Sure, it was machismo, but it still made him proud. He popped his head in his boss's office on the way to his cubicle.

"Steve, I lost a couple of clients—to the Grim Reaper," he said.

"Okay, I should be in most of the day. Run the policies by me when you can."

Steve Miller was new to the Richmond office, and a good boss who had "been there and done that" with the company for years. Miller had taken over just four months after Mike started with the company. Mike liked him and like everyone else, much preferred him to Justin Stolzheimer, the guy who had been there before.

Stolzheimer was a nerdy, bespectacled, mouse-like number cruncher with absolutely no charisma and no personality. He knew very little about management, Mike had found, and absolutely nothing about leadership. Stolzheimer clearly had the mistaken impression that he was always the smartest person in the room. Numerous others had a different opinion.

Stolzheimer turned out to be a back-stabbing, insecure bureaucrat who had started out as a certified public accountant and should have remained one. He had been promoted beyond his abilities simply because he was a number cruncher who could handle a budget. In fact, he'd worked in and eventually headed up Archer's Budget Department before being advanced by the organization's leaders. Virtually no one liked him, and everyone talked about him behind his back, almost unanimously agreeing on what a joke he was. It probably was a good thing he was gone, Mike thought. He wasn't sure he wouldn't want to deck him some day.

Nobody but the corporate higher-ups thought Stolzheimer belonged in his position and there was a universal sigh of relief when Archer replaced him. Miller was a big improvement, but then again, anyone would have been.

"Leadership," Mike thought with a smirk. What passed for leadership here in the civilian world made him laugh. He had worked for many Marines, including several generals, whom he'd willingly have followed into Hell and back.

Moreover, he was confident they'd get him through the round trip. Most of the narcissistic, self-impressed people he'd met since he got out of the Corps—guys like Stolzheimer—a nerd who flattered himself by thinking he was a leader just by virtue of the position he held—couldn't lead a troop of Cub Scouts into a K-Mart and back out again. The difference between a leader and a manager did not seem evident to most civilians—if to any—he thought.

And that went especially for the previous Commander- in-Chief, a president with virtually no prior experience leading anything except "community activists." Like most Marines he knew, to him, that joker was a national embarrassment. He was glad he was finally gone, too. Mike subconsciously shook his head.

He knew so many Marines who would clearly do a far better job in the White House than some of the presidents the public had elected over the past few terms. The new guy had promise...rough around the edges maybe, but at least someone with a love of country and extensive experience running large corporations. He was as divisive as his predecessor, maybe even more so, but for different reasons. But, he was a successful businessman who had become a billionaire. Maybe it was time for someone to run the country like a business...time would tell.

There was nothing in the Richmond Times-Dispatch obituaries yet for Trumbull. Probably tomorrow. Bill Wilford's would most likely be in the Fredericksburg paper. But there was already a very brief mention of Marvin Kincaid and a small photo of him in his Army uniform. It just seemed so screwed up that such a young man, who had served his country, had a great family, and so much to live for, was gone.

No cause of death was listed. "Final arrangements by L. G. Bristow Funeral Home, family will receive friends Wednesday night from 7-9." He put it on his calendar on his iPhone. It just pissed him off to think about it.

———※———

The next two days were fairly routine at work. He needed a few things, so he did some brief shopping for groceries at the Kroger supermarket after work on Tuesday and headed home for a night of TV—mostly "The American Heroes Channel" and the local news, as usual.

He wasn't fond of much of the network stuff on what he derisively called "the idiot box." He generally got most of his news right off of his cell phone or by listening to the radio as he drove. He also favored magazines—lots of them, from Popular Science and Popular Mechanics to a host of military publications. But TV was a good diversion now and then, if there was some programming that interested him. Tonight, there was a good history of the fighting in Fallujah. He had missed that one when he was on active duty, but it was a hell of a battle as U.S. forces fought house-to-house there.

After a quick dinner of Spanish rice from a can and some frozen burritos, chased down with a cold Budweiser, it was time to grab the remote.

C H A P T E R

4

Kimberly

He'd only had the show on for 10 minutes when the phone rang. He paused the TV. He didn't want to miss the rest of the Fallujah documentary.

"Hello."

"Hey Mike, just thinking about you and figured I'd check in. How's everything?" said a soft voice that he recognized instantly.

"Hi, Good Looking! It's great to hear from you! How are you? What's new with you?"

"I'm good. I'm moving into my new place and still lugging boxes around. I wish you were here to help!"

"Me, too."

"So, how are things in Richmond?"

"Aw, they've been better. I had a couple of clients die, and one of them was a good friend. I know the family really well and there are three young kids... just really sad. I'm kinda bummed at the moment."

"I'm sorry. If I were there, I could help you forget about it."

"Well, maybe not forget, but certainly deal with it a lot better than I am. I miss you." A smile happened. He couldn't help it when he talked with Kimberly.

"Ditto."

"So, do I have to call you 'Doctor Sheffield' now that you have that pharmacology degree?"

"Absolutely!" She laughed as she said it.

"Well, I'm proud of you. That was a lot of work and I think you've picked a great career field. I know your parents must be busting their buttons."

"Yeah, mom's really excited about it, and I think dad's most happy that I moved to Chicago near them. He's very protective of me."

"That's right--now that he's with Bell-Boeing, how is he enjoying retirement from the Marines?"

"You know all about that—you can take the Marine out of the Marine Corps, but you can't take the Corps out of the Marine…what you guys call, "Once a Marine, Always a Marine!""

"It's true. I think about it every day, and I miss it. I think I'll miss it until I die."

"My dad says Marines never die, they just go to Hell and regroup!"

Mike laughed.

"Yeah. He's right about that. We also used to say that Heaven doesn't want us, and Hell is afraid we'll take over! On the other hand, the Marines' Hymn says that the gates to Heaven are guarded by United States Marines, so who knows?"

Bell-Boeing had its headquarters in Chicago. The company developed the revolutionary Osprey aircraft, which can take off and land like a helicopter, but then tilt its rotors and fly straight like a fixed-wing aircraft. It gave the Marines the ability to launch off ships farther out at sea when assaulting a beachhead or points behind enemy lines.

The Osprey flew faster, farther and carried a heavier payload than many of the helicopters in the inventory. Some of the other services were now using it as well.

Coming out of the aviation field in the Corps, Major General Sheffield was a natural for the company, once he'd waited the required period of time so that there would not be any perceived issues of undue influence or other improprieties. He'd now be continuing to work on the Osprey project—improvements to its capabilities, new missions, etc. Nobody could do it better.

"Of course your dad is protective of you. You're his only daughter. I'd be the same way. So, what do you think of your job so far?"

"I think it's going to be pretty good. I got hired by a research lab here and while I have a lot to learn, it's going to be a lot more exciting than working at Walgreens!"

"Hey, don't bad mouth Walgreens—I get some prescriptions filled there sometimes! In fact, I've even done quick food shopping there a couple of times. They have the basics—and frozen pizza and ice cream. What more could you want?"

"Yeah, real gourmet stuff, huh?"

"It's not like I buy ALL my food there. But sometimes you're picking up a prescription and you say, 'What the heck, it's pizza!'"

They talked for the next half hour, and Mike was glad to reconnect. Now that she was in Chicago and a short hop by plane from Richmond, maybe they could get together again sometime.

Talking with Kimberly (and she didn't like the shorter, "Kim,") Mike had thought back to how they'd met and to all that had happened in both of their lives since. Still, here they were, years later, still in touch and still caring about each other.

While he thought of her often, he was always pleasantly surprised that she had not met someone and gotten married by now. She was so pretty, smart, and also articulate, which Mike had found was a quality lacking in a lot of the women he'd dated...but she was probably too career-focused to want to muddle things up with a serious, committed relationship, he thought.

After graduating from Virginia Commonwealth University, commonly shortened to VCU in Richmond, Mike had gone to Officer Candidate School at Marine Corps Base, Quantico, Virginia, just up I-95 North about an hour from Richmond. He then attended The Basic School, the 6-month-long course for all new Marine lieutenants, followed by the Basic Communication Officers School, also located there on the more than 55,000-acre base, for the next few months.

While attending Comm. School, he had met Kimberly one day at the PX when he dropped his checkbook without being aware of it. She had picked it up and followed him through the store to return it. "Chivalry in reverse," he'd said at the time, smiling.

"Somebody has to take care of our Marines," Kimberly had said.

Being a hard-charging young Marine lieutenant, he did what any hard-charging young Marine lieutenant would do, and asked the cute young lady to join him for a soda and maybe a slice of pizza in the attached cafeteria.

The lady had fortunately said yes, and the conversation flowed well until Kimberly mentioned that her dad was a pilot, a colonel, and worked at the base.

In fact, he was the commanding officer of HMX-1, the president's famous Marine helicopter unit. It was almost too much for Mike to take in. At that time, Kimberly was home from school on a break from Temple University in Philadelphia, where she was taking pharmacology courses.

The fact that her dad was a very senior officer with such an important job made Mike more than a bit apprehensive. Colonels are a big deal in the Marines—especially to brand new 2nd lieutenants. On top of that, you can't get much more important as a colonel than to be in charge of the president's helicopters.

"Well, thanks again," he said. "I'd have starved if you hadn't returned my checkbook.' That really wasn't true, since he could always get his meals at the Dining Facility...still the "Mess Hall" to most Marines, during training, but he did stock up on snacks, and it seemed like a good thing to say to let her know he appreciated her for tracking him down to return it.

"No problem, thanks for the pizza. Good luck with the rest of your training. It was great meeting you." Kimberly left in a flutter of fabric and a wisp of sweet fragrance that lingered in Mike's mind for the rest of the day.

C H A P T E R

Quantico, Virginia

Mike didn't see Kimberly after that for months. He didn't really expect to ever see her again. In the interim she'd gone back to school in Philadelphia and he was back out in the tick-infested woods of Quantico—and in the class-rooms—learning how to provide reliable, secure radio and telephone communications in a tactical situation.

Just like at Officer Candidate School and The Basic School, training was rigorous and challeng-ing. Going through OCS when he was on summer break from VCU, he'd started in a platoon of 51 men. Ten weeks later, he was one of only 22 who graduated.

Sure, Marine Corps physical requirements are tough. But a lot of it was a mind game, he'd thought. The regular officers and non-commissioned officers who trained the aspiring officer candidates knew a lot of tricks that deliberately tested the candidates' ability to handle stress. Their goal was to weed out the guys who couldn't cut it here, before they ended up getting themselves and their Marines killed someplace else.

He remembered digging one time for the better part of two hours in the thick, red Virginia clay with his entrenching tool, getting set up where another lieutenant in an assigned leadership role had told him to dig for a 3-day tactical field exercise. When he was almost finished, his hands literally bleeding and calloused, the other lieutenant came over and told him that the tactical situation had changed and he needed to go dig a new fighting hole on the other side of the perimeter.

In one of many philosophical differences, the Marines call them fighting holes, while the Army traditionally has called them foxholes.

Marines fight, they don't run and hide like foxes, he'd been taught. "Aggression, attack, kill"...these were characteristics that were scorned, feared and derided—even punished—in the civilian world. But these were desired, no...essential traits, in America's Marines.

The Marine Corps was not a social club, nor a social experiment. It was about wanting peace but being 100 percent willing to stick a bayonet and twist it in someone who is attacking our country and threatening our families and our way of life. Freedom isn't free, Mike thought to himself on more than one occasion.

It has been said that a soldier will shoot the enemy, but a Marine will shoot him and then stick a bayonet in the bullet hole for extra points. Being a Marine wasn't for everyone. There was a warrior ethos that was inculcated, nurtured, reinforced and expected...no... demanded. It was an imperceptible code that every Marine abided by.

Now, unhappy about all the work he'd done for nothing digging this fighting hole, he had cursed audibly and failed to impress a nearby captain with an instant willingness to comply, and soon was doing push-ups and running up and down a nearby hill until he thought he'd black out.

The captain, a decorated Vietnam veteran with visible scars on his chest and arms attesting to the reasons for his Purple Heart, had told Mike in no uncertain terms that he would personally "...take you out in the woods and kick your ass next time" if he saw him fail to comply with another student leader's orders again. While Mike knew that was against the rules, he wasn't entirely sure the captain would care about that. Message received!

The daily physical grind in training was hard. He had expected that, of course, and had prepared himself before he started OCS by running, lifting weights and doing push-ups, but there simply was no way to be adequately prepared for Marine Corps training. The emotional stress, constant yelling, being berated and sheer exhaustion were difficulties piled on top of the physical challenges. What he hated the most, though, was the long marches—14 miles once—fully loaded with a pack, rifle, canteens and more, all in the Virginia summer heat.

One day, it was 94 degrees and humid. While his platoon was supposedly "acclimated" by now, he was one of the few in his squad of 13 who didn't end up at sick bay from the heat and the strain, or the blisters. He felt sick and had blisters, too, but was determined not to drop out of the march. Quite a few candidates dropped off along the way. Navy corpsmen driving small motorized vehicles called mules picked them up and took them away for treatment.

———

A few hours after that march, he had looked at his feet and found them to be bleeding and missing large chunks of skin. He wore two pairs of socks the next day and refrained from asking to go to "Sick Bay" to be treated.

It was clear to Mike that the instructors did everything the candidates did, and more. Carrying their own packs, they literally ran up and down the trails, urging the candidates to keep moving. Those guys were just piles of steel and stone, the candidates agreed.

Two years later, after graduating from college in Richmond and now back at Quantico, this time at the Basic School as a lieutenant instead of as an officer candidate, a young officer was treated with more respect, but the training was more challenging than ever.

The academics, in fact, were much harder than Mike's college courses. First of all, you were tired all the time from all the physical activity. Mike learned everything from small-unit tactics, to handling a wide range of semiautomatic and automatic weapons, to hand-to-hand combat, first aid, camouflage techniques, topography and land navigation...and much more.

Military schools throw so much information at students in such a short amount of time, that it's often been compared to trying to get a drink from a fire hose.

Besides all that, learning to plot and call in artillery or mortar fire or bombardments from U.S. Navy vessels just didn't come naturally to Mike.

He had no idea that math was going to be such a big part of his training here. He hated math in High School and took only the one required course in college. He hated it then and he hated it now. But now, his career, and ultimately maybe his life, could depend on it.

In retrospect, a lot of it was fun. Mike got to fire

the 9 millimeter and .45 caliber service pistols, the M-19 automatic grenade launcher, the LAAW (Light Anti-Tank Assault Weapon), the 12-gauge shotgun, and of course the M-16 service rifle, among other weapons. No matter their specialty, every Marine is a rifleman, Mike remembered being taught.

Training with the M-16 was boring at first. Instructors set out barrels at various distances. The barrels had small silhouettes of "man shaped" targets painted on them.

These resembled the actual, full-sized targets the lieutenants would soon shoot at on the range, at distances of 200, 300 and 500 yards...greater distances than any of the other branches of the U.S. military. First, though, they would spend hours... many hours... "snapping in."

This entailed sighting in, without firing, on the barrels while in various positions...prone, kneeling and standing. Instructors harped on proper technique, use of the rifle's sling for stability, etc. The practice also honed what the instructors called "muscle memory," which helped shooters to automatically slip into correct firing positions after much practice.

Snapping in, and later, actually firing the rifle, took on almost a mystical quality. Marines would wear the same uniform—dirty—day after day, to have the same "feel" about the marksmanship process. That transferred from snapping in to the range when live firing began.

It was almost a superstition that if you changed your clothes, or God forbid, washed them, you'd change your "dope," or the qualities of your preparation, and therefore, your accuracy. All this was part of the lore that, "The Marines train the world's best marksmen."

During fighting in France during World War I, Germans nicknamed America's Marines "Teufel Hunden," or "Devil Dogs," largely because they were astounded that Marines fought so ferociously and were routinely picking German soldiers off at ranges of up to 1,000 yards when they poked their heads up out of the trenches they were in.

All the training was hard. No mistake about it. Somehow, though, the camaraderie and the pride in being a Marine officer made it all worthwhile. Mike enjoyed it and felt more physically fit and more capable overall than he ever had in his life.

Besides the lifetime pride and sense of accomplishment he'd earned as a Marine officer, he'd also gotten to see some exotic places and meet a lot of interesting people, including a pretty Air Force lieutenant during a 1-year tour in Okinawa, Japan.

Cindy was a pleasant distraction for a while, but not the one he wanted to end up with someday. He was a conservative in pretty much every way. Cindy was too liberal and they didn't agree on most important things.

But, among Marines, the commonly accepted theory was that the best-looking women in the military were in the Air Force. Whether that was true or not, Cindy certainly fit the bill...tall, blonde and leggy. The attraction was almost entirely physical, and mutual.

She was an air traffic controller at Kadena Air Base and they spent a lot of time at Tiger Beach, Moon Beach and other popular Okinawan recreational areas, and often met at the Officers Club at Kadena for drinks and bar food. He liked her, and she was fun--but then there was Kimberly...always in the back of his mind. He kept thinking that he wanted to try to get together with her when he returned to "stateside," as it was known here on this tiny island.

When he had unexpectedly seen Kimberly again after their first meeting at the PX a couple of years ago at Quantico, he was at the base bowling center with two other lieutenants when Kimberly showed up with a group. He noticed her settling in at a lane and picking out a ball, testing each one as she lifted it for weight and a good fit to her hand, which he noticed had long, delicate fingers.

He remembered her as being attractive, but on this particular evening she looked even better than he recalled. Her chestnut hair was different somehow, maybe darker, and she had on a bright blue top that looked great on her. He noticed her shape in it and grinned subconsciously. She was hot.

It was a while before she saw him, but when she did, she waved and motioned for him to come over to say hello. He was a bit surprised that she had recognized him. All the lieutenants, with their short hair cuts, looked a lot alike.

"Be back in a few, guys," he said. "Let me know when it's my turn."

"Whoa, DePalma—very nice!" one of the lieutenants said, noticing the object of Mike's attention.

Mike walked the few yards to lane 16 and said, "Hi, I didn't know you were a bowler."

"I'm definitely not," she laughed. But, my dad is, so my family is here. "Mom, Dad, this is Mike. Mike, this is my mom, dad, and my brothers, Zach and Phillip."

Boom, it hit him. "Dad" was the colonel.

"Good evening, Sir,…Ma'am," he said. "I'm Lieutenant DePalma." "Good evening, guys," he said, shaking hands with the boys. He was not about to shake the colonel's hand, and the colonel didn't offer it. Then again, he was holding a bowling ball at the time.

"How do you know Kimberly?" the colonel asked.

"Sir, she rescued me at the PX a few months ago when I lost my checkbook and she found it," Mike said, looking the colonel in the eye as he knew a Marine officer should.

Colonel Glenn Sheffield was exactly what a Marine colonel is supposed to look like…lean but solidly built, with a "high and tight" haircut that showed glimmers of gray on the sides. His facial features were strong and he had an air of capability about him…that indefinable presence of confidence that Marines acquire.

"You're lucky." I can't get my checkbook away from her mother."

Mike smiled and relaxed a little. At least the colonel had a sense of humor.

Mike and Kimberly made small talk about bowling and were just getting comfortable talking with each other again.

"DePalma—you're up!" one of his buddies yelled.

"Excuse me, please, Sir. I have to go show these two lieutenants how it's done. Nice to meet you Sir,…Ma'am. Good luck bowling, guys. Good to see you again, Kimberly," Mike said, turning to leave.

"You, too," Kimberly said, unexpectedly extending her hand to shake Mike's. He gripped her hand gently. It felt warm and soft and he didn't want to let go, but did so even as he eventually realized he'd clearly held it for longer than required for a polite goodbye.

About 15 minutes later, when he noticed that Kimberly had gone to the snack bar for a drink and was away from the colonel, Mike went up to order something too. He didn't want anything, but it was the perfect opportunity to ask for her phone number, which she gave him with a smile that he'd remember for a long time.

After a couple of days, so as not to look too eager, Mike gave her a call late one afternoon and was lucky. She answered the phone, sparing him the stress of having to talk to the colonel or the colonel's wife.

———

There wasn't much to do around Quantico, or in Triangle, right outside the gate, but there was a decent movie playing in Woodbridge, nearby. Mike asked for a date, and Kimberly agreed. He picked her up in the ugly, mustard-color Plymouth he drove at the time and drove more carefully than he ever had. First of all, she was really nice-looking, smelled good, and was very distracting. Secondly, there was the nagging matter of the colonel.

And so began a short-lived relationship. Short-lived because Kimberly had another two years of college and would soon be leaving the base, and he'd be on his way to wherever the Marine Corps decided to send him after Communication School. But, they saw each other a few times before he left Quantico, whenever she was home on a holiday or semester break.

He didn't get too much time off from training, but usually had a couple of hours on the weekend. He remained respectful—scared of the colonel, frankly—but they finally got a bit beyond the kiss goodnight stage after a few dates. Neither of them was ready to take the relationship all the way, sexually. Kimberly was reserved. Mike was still petrified of the colonel. He figured maybe Kimberly was, too. Still, it was pretty awesome!

He missed her when she left for school again, but he had gotten orders for Okinawa anyway, and would be gone for a year. It didn't seem that they'd probably see each other again. They did exchange letters a couple of times during the next year, and a photo or two. He figured some preppie college guy would have Kimberly all wrapped up by now, though.

C H A P T E R

Okinawa, Japan

Okinawa is a common duty station for Marines. South of Japan and situated in the East China Sea, Okinawa is only about 65 miles long and a few miles wide. It holds an important place in Marine Corps history and was the site of a ferocious battle in 1945 between the Marines and Japanese forces as the Pacific island-hopping campaign drew U.S. World War II forces closer and closer to the Japanese mainland.

The island had been so fortified by the emperor's troops that Japanese generals had bragged that a million men could not seize Okinawa in a thousand years. Marines, along with the U.S. Tenth Army Division, took the heavily fortified island in three months of intense fighting. Today, American bases on the island include Army, Air Force, Navy and Marine personnel. The U.S. Coast Guard's 11th Regional station also is headquartered there in the port city of Naha.

Mike settled in to a B.O.Q. -- Bachelor Officers Quarters-- and immediately was busy leading a platoon in 7th Communication Battalion. Living in the BOQ here was different, for sure. He shared an adjoining bathroom with another officer. An Okinawan Mama San, as they were known here, provided cleaning and laundry services for the two officers, as well as for others in the BOQ.

Mike could come in out of the field with muddy boots, sweaty camouflage utilities and his undershirt and underwear, throw them all in a heap on the floor, and come back later to spit-shined boots, heavily starched cammies and laundered undergarments. A guy could get spoiled.

Once, when he was in the shower that was located between the two officers' rooms, the old Mama San accidentally...maybe... walked in on him as she prepared to clean the shower. He was instantly embarrassed and defensive but Mama San simply smiled and bowed slightly. She had been cleaning BOQs for years. Seeing a showering Marine was nothing new to her.

After about two months, he and his platoon got orders to board a Navy ship, the amphibious cargo ship U.S.S. St. Louis, for a training operation that would take them to the Philippines, Singapore and other areas.

Aboard ship, training consisted of routine maintenance on communications equipment and some classes Mike held on the Uniform Code of Military Justice--military law--and tactics, First Aid and other basics his Marines needed to stay schooled up on.

The Marines did calisthenics, repeatedly lifted anything heavy they could find, and ran around the main deck and exercised everyplace they could, usually yelling "OOH-RAH, MARINE CORPS!" as they did so, driving the sailors somewhat crazy.

Olongapo, Philippines

Olongapo, near Subic Bay in the Philippines, was a wild place. Alcohol flowed freely in the bars, most of which had an affinity, for some reason, for bands made up of young Filipino guys playing U.S. Country Western music. Quite a few Marines and sailors found themselves hooking up with friendly local girls. Some of those arrangements went smoothly and led to very happy troops. Many involved the transfer of cash, chocolate, M.R.E.s (Meal, Ready to Eat) or other goods. The people here were largely poor and it was sad how little it took for an American serviceman to buy affection, or what passed for it here.

Similarly, Mike had watched some of the troops throw coins into a muddy creek filled with trash. They called it, "Shit River." The coins enticed local boys to dive into the muck to retrieve them. It was really sad and Mike felt bad for the kids. He gave some of them a few bucks or a chocolate bar once in a while, with no diving required. Their eyes grew wide with disbelief and gratitude when he handed them cash with no request that they do anything for it. The only problem was that once he flashed cash, a flock of kids would swarm him, playing "pat-pat" as they tried to grab his wallet or anything in his pockets. The kind of poverty that drove this type of behavior was numbing to Mike.

Other interactions between the troops and the girls in town at times led to the Marines and sailors getting robbed or contracting unpleasant "social diseases" that the Navy corpsmen addressed with a variety of medications and other even more unpleasant treatments, including the dreaded "bore punch."

Mike, like many of the officers and senior enlisted men, used his liberty time ashore to do a little shopping. This is not to say that some of them didn't engage in the same activities as the enlisted men, but at least in Mike's case, he was not drawn to the bars too often and avoided the local women. He had heard all the stories and it seemed too seedy to him. Other than having a beer, making sure it came in an unopened bottle, he was willing to avoid all that until he got to see Cindy again. The cruise had to end sometime, he thought.

He picked up a bit of jewelry and some carved "monkey pod" wooden items he thought his mom would like, but nothing too large, since he had very little room aboard ship to keep anything. He picked up a necklace he thought Cindy would like. He also bought a large Marine Corps Eagle, Globe and Anchor wall plaque carved out of the native monkey pod wood. Someday, that would look good in a den.

During the day, the jungle and beaches provided excellent training venues for the embarked Marines. Mike had his troops practice extensively with radio and wire communications, including making "field expedient" antennas out of various materials, including black "slash wire" wound around a helmet. They also practiced tactics like patrolling and setting up a secure defensive perimeter.

Soon, the Marines went back aboard ship and sailed away from the Philippines. It had been good to get onto solid ground for a while, but the sooner they finished this tour, the sooner they'd be back on Okinawa, counting down the days to return "stateside."

Next, Singapore and two other more remote ports awaited prior to the return to Okinawa. Singapore provided more good training, especially the opportunity to work with Singapore troops, who were sharp and good at what they did. They impressed Mike and he learned from them as they did from him and his Marines.

C H A P T E R

Camp LeJeune, North Carolina

Soon, even though it seemed like forever, his Pacific cruise and his 12-month-long Okinawa tour was over. He said goodbye to Cindy and headed stateside, this time to Camp LeJeune, North Carolina. Cindy was a sexy girl and they shared some interests, but despite both being in the military, those interests weren't enough to build a relationship lasting longer than the year spent together on Okinawa.

He and Cindy were a hot item for a while, but ended up mainly as "friends with benefits" before he left for the states. They had exchanged phone numbers, but he doubted whether they would connect again once he left the island, figuratively or literally.

Meanwhile, Kimberly had finished another year at Temple University in Philadelphia, closing in on a doctoral degree in Pharmacology, she wrote. Her dad had been selected for promotion to brigadier general, she told Mike, and was being transferred to the West Coast. Mike was not surprised, and was happy to hear about the promotion, as he'd come to like her dad when he'd gotten to know him a little better. But, Mike and Kimberly didn't see each other right away when he first got back to the states.

About a month after returning to the states, Mike was promoted to 1st lieutenant and it seemed like he might possibly make a career of the Marines. He liked it, and felt privileged to wear the famous Marine Corps Eagle, Globe and Anchor and to lead young Marines. He loved the camaraderie and the sense of adventure he felt as a Marine. The pay raise he got with his promotion also was welcome.

For the next year and a half, he led his platoon's training, both in garrison and on various field exercises. His experience in Okinawa and in the Philippines and Singapore while on his cruise, training and practicing, had honed his skills. He imparted his knowledge to his platoon at Camp LeJeune.

Some of his corporals and sergeants, the Non-Commissioned Officers, were very proficient with the equipment, and taught the newer Marines as well. He knew that if they were called upon to provide dependable tactical communications anyplace in the world, they could do it, and do it with almost no advance notice. They were ready.

He mostly enjoyed the time at LeJeune. The Officers Club was a great place to have a few beers, enjoy some snacks or a burger and talk with other Marines. The nearby beaches were a great place to go on liberty, and he had a few dates with some of the local girls. Jacksonville, right outside the gate, was a typical military town. It offered grocery stores, gas stations, used car dealerships, pawn shops and tattoo parlors. And yes, bars. Lots of bars.

He liked seafood, and there were a couple of good places where you could go and get shrimp and freshly caught fish right off the boat. Every once in a while, he'd make the drive to Morehead City to eat at the locally famous Sanitary Restaurant. The name, he had learned, went way back to a time when such things as sanitary food preparation were not taken for granted.

As Wire Platoon commander at Camp LeJeune's Communications Company, part of the 2d Force Service Support Group, he led young Marines responsible for setting up field telephone communications. He had found out only recently that 2D FSSG was renamed 2nd Marine Logistics Group since he left the Corps.

In a tactical situation where radios are used for many communications, there always is a concern about transmissions being jammed or intercepted. Staying ahead of potential enemies' ability to tap into conversations is a constant challenge technologically. But in the field, wire can be strung from unit to unit, providing secure communications behind a safe perimeter.

While black field communications wire, called "slash wire" for some reason by Marines, might seem obsolete in an age of digital wireless communications, modern field switchboards are a thing of amazing capability—a far cry from the World War II systems that were used by the Greatest Generation, Mike knew.

He enjoyed the work, and had some really sharp Non-Commissioned Officers working for him. These NCO's, the corporals and sergeants, were young men and women who wanted to lead their fellow Marines. They had proved themselves worthy of promotion in a highly competitive environment, and had the technical knowledge and growing leadership experience that Mike depended on. He seldom had to correct one of his Marines for any slip-up in discipline or judgment, because his NCO's were instantly on top of any such infractions, which were few and far between. His platoon was a smoothly operating machine.

One morning, as Mike approached the headquarters building, several young Marines were seated on the steps, relaxing. All of them jumped to attention to salute him and say, "Good morning, Sir!" as is customary in the Corps. All but one.

Mike had not even noticed, because that Marine, not one of his, was off to the side and out of his peripheral vision's field of view. Suddenly, a staff sergeant came running out of one of the offices. He had observed the lieutenant's approach and saw that the one Marine had apparently deliberately avoided saluting the officer. Mike was embarrassed hearing the sergeant chewing out the offending Marine, but he understood the need for discipline and he knew the Marine Corps is much more inclined to enforce it than some of the other branches of the military. In fact, a Marine could be "written up" and fined, demoted or even incarcerated for what some might consider minor infractions. He continued and entered the building, later thanking the staff sergeant for handling the situation so well.

While Mike was at LeJeune, Brigadier General Sheffield had not surprisingly been picked up for a second star. He was highly regarded in the Corps, especially among the aviators. A skilled pilot and born leader, he had advanced quickly, even being selected for Major General above some of his peers who had more time in grade.

His HMX-1 tour no doubt had been a factor in that, Mike thought. The Corps was small and elite when compared to the other U.S. military forces, and only had fewer than 70 general officers in total, so everybody in the officer corps knew when the generals got promoted. Teletype messages were sent out Corps-wide with such announcements.

Mike was happy for the Sheffields, and happy to be a part of an organization with men and women like the general and his own NCOs and Staff Non-Commissioned Officers. The Staff NCOs were the Marines with ranks from staff sergeant up through sergeant major and master gunnery sergeant (E-9) ranks. These were the men and women with the extensive military knowledge and experience that the officers relied on most heavily.

Mike was content. He had a decent car, sharp uniforms, money in his pocket and a career he enjoyed and was proud of. All in all, it was a good time in his life. Things changed one rainy night on a dark rural road outside Wilmington, North Carolina, when a drunk driver hydroplaned, crossed the double yellow line, and slammed into Mike's car.

Mike had driven down to see the battleship U.S.S. North Carolina, moored there. He had spent hours touring the ship and talking with the men and women who were aboard to assist visitors.

He was heading back to LeJeune, taking his time because of the weather. He'd seen the oncoming vehicle's headlights speeding toward him and had just enough time to steer to the side to avoid a full head-on collision, but he got hit hard and his car was totaled.

The other driver, a 19-year old girl, had some fractures and bruises, as did Mike, but Mike's back also was broken on impact and despite good care and months of recuperation, it became obvious to him, and to the Navy doctors at Camp LeJeune, that the physicality and rigors of Marine Corps life were going to be impossible to bear after his multiple surgeries.

The passenger in the car driven by the teenager had life-threatening injuries and facial scarring she'd carry forever. She ultimately survived, but was forever crippled. It was an experience they all could have done without.

Reluctantly, Mike eventually accepted an Honorable Discharge for medical reasons, and moved back to Richmond, Virginia.

He clearly remembered talking with the Marine Recruiter at the Officer Selection Office when he had walked in during his college years, just to get some information. He remembered the young Marine captain he spoke with telling him that even a couple of years in the Corps would get him in the best shape of his life and give him excellent resume content for the future. That all had proved to be true.

And, said the captain, anyone who stayed in until retirement would get lifetime benefits, including health care, free prescription medications and a pension.

It had all sounded great to Mike. It was what he planned to do—make a career of the Marine Corps. Now, he was disheartened and unsure of what to do next. He had completed a resume, filled out a few applications and started networking with everyone he knew who might be able to help him get started on a new career.

Mike had some savings, but he needed to find a job soon. Fortunately, he still had quite a few contacts in the Richmond area. A couple of interviews had seemed promising, but for one reason or another, didn't work out, either because he didn't get offered a position, or the pay or work specifics didn't seem like a good fit to him.

One friend he'd made while a student at VCU now worked for Archer Global Life, a large insurance company with a regional office in the city. He told Mike that a man with the kind of initiative the Marines inculcated into its members could be very successful with the company. He arranged for Mike to get an interview, which led to a job offer and the requisite training to become an insurance agent for the company.

Mike installed a pull-up bar in a doorway in his new apartment, and between that and sit-ups, push-ups and doing some at first 1, then 2 and 3-mile easy runs around some of the city's historic sites, he stayed in good shape and gradually regained his strength.

Other than having some back pain if he did any heavy lifting, he generally felt better than he'd thought he would after finishing rehab at LeJeune. He wore an elastic back brace on bad days. It helped a bit. Good running shoes were a must. He popped lots of ibuprofen, but figured that was a small price to pay to be able to keep active.

He had graduated from VCU with a degree in Business Administration and had joined the Marines because he wanted to travel and see the world while serving with what he perceived to be the most respected and challenging of the military services. He had done that and was proud of it.

Fate had stepped in and decided it was time for him to do something else. He didn't know what God had in store for him, but now it was time to settle into a second career. He would be a U.S. Marine until his dying day, but now, he was also an Archer Global man.

C H A P T E R

Farewell

Nearly a week had passed since Marvin had passed away.

As he neared the funeral home where Marv's family waited to welcome friends, Mike had a sharp pain in the pit of his stomach. He didn't know how he'd face his friend's wife and kids. The sadness he felt was deep and searing.

He parked the Mercedes in the crowded parking lot and made his way into the room where Marv was laid out. The casket was open and several people were standing together, reminiscing about their experiences with Marv. The many floral tributes that had been sent by family and friends filled the large room with their fragrance. In the casket, Marv looked young and natural, like a man taking a quick nap after an hour of tossing a football around with his kids.

Photos of Marv were displayed on a long, wooden table up against one wall. In some, he was wearing his Army uniform. Others showed him playing football with his sons. There were a couple of him fishing. As Mike looked at them, he felt a mixture of happiness and sadness. Marv had enjoyed a great family, hobbies and a lot of love.

Nearby, Cathy stood with people offering their sympathy and Mike saw the boys sitting in the front of the room with family members, presumably from both Cathy's family and Marv's. A low murmur filled the room as people talked in hushed tones, punctuated occasionally by laughter as someone remembered something funny that Marv had said or done.

He made his way near Cathy, who was talking with a tall, white-haired woman. When she could, Cathy reached out for Mike and he hugged her. She was holding it together as well as could be expected, but clearly had been crying.

"I'm so sorry, Cathy. I'm just shocked. How are you doing?"

"I'm trying, Mike. I have to be strong for the boys, but it's not easy. I'm still in shock too. It was just so sudden and unexpected."

"I know. I can't imagine what you're dealing with. I'll get with you in a day or two and talk about business then. I'll call you, okay?"

"Thanks, Mike. You were a good friend to Marv, and he really liked you a lot."

"Yeah. I felt the same. This is a tough time. I'll do whatever I can to help you, and I know everyone else will, too. Please call me once in a while and let me know how you and the kids are doing." He hugged her and made his way through the crowded room.

He hugged Andrew, Nicholas and Jason. Andrew looked stoic, but Nicholas had tears rolling down his face and Jason was snuggled up against Cathy's mom, sobbing quietly. It was painful to see

Marv's boys so sad and to be powerless to do anything about it. He shook hands with a few others
who had come to pay their respects, and sought out
Marv's parents to pay his condolences to them, then
signed the guest book, took an "In Memoriam" card,
and walked out into the darkness, feeling older.

10

The Check

One of Archer Global's administrative assistants walked in to see Mike and laid some folders on his desk. One of them contained Marv Kincaid's policy, some endorsements signed by his boss, and a check. Sad as it would be to deliver it, he knew that Cathy could use the money. After the funeral was paid for, there'd be plenty left to pay off the family's mortgage, some miscellaneous bills and all college expenses as the boys grew. He was glad that Marv had asked him to increase the coverage when he did. He also liked to think that their friendship played a part in Marv's decision.

He called Cathy to arrange a convenient time for him to visit. She suggested three days later, after the burial, as the older boys would be in school, and the little one would be having a play date with a neighborhood friend at the friend's house, allowing time to talk.

"Works for me, Cathy. I'll see you tomorrow at the cemetery, and then we can meet in a couple of days to go over the policy premium.' He heard himself say "cemetery," and wished he had somehow rephrased what he said. It was such a sad word and he felt it pound his heart.

"Thanks," she said. Mike heard the heaviness in her voice. It would be a difficult but necessary conversation to have.

At the cemetery, Mike stood among the friends and family at the burial site, said a silent prayer, and hugged Cathy, but didn't spend much time with her. His heart hurt too much. He hugged the boys and told them their dad loved them very much and that he was an American hero. Then, he left.

The next day, he drove to the house and rang the doorbell. Cathy opened the door, immediately hugging him.

"It's so good to see you. Come on in," she said, obviously trying to hold back tears.

"I'm sorry. I'll try not to cry," she said.

"It's okay. You don't need to do that for me. I'm a friend."

They talked about the viewing and the burial and old times. After a while, Mike handed her the check and she took it, her hand shaking.

"Cathy, do you know anything yet for sure from the doctors about what happened?"

"Not really. He was on a couple of medications for some atrial fibrillation he had a few times, but I don't think his doctor thought he had any really serious conditions that weren't being managed with his prescriptions."

"Well, sometimes there's just no explanation, I guess, but we always want answers, don't we?"

"I suppose it wouldn't change anything," Cathy said, looking out the window at the trees swaying in her yard.

"Cathy, about the check...as you know, Mike had just recently increased his coverage. I don't know why he did, but I'm glad for you and the boys."

"Thanks. This will help." She dabbed a tissue at a tear as she took the check.

11

A Puzzle

Weeks had gone by, and he'd called twice to check in on Cathy and the boys. He also stopped by once to throw a football around with the boys, as he had when he'd visited with Marv. It just wasn't the same, for him or Marv's boys. Cathy was doing what she could to restore a sense of normalcy to the family, but their dad was missing and the boys would miss him terribly for the rest of their lives.

Eventually, the weeks turned into a couple of months, and Mike's job with Archer Global Life was going well. He was selling quite a few policies and expanding his growing network of contacts in and around Richmond.

One day, he was reading the **Richmond Times-Dispatch** when a headline caught his eye.

VETERAN DEATH RATES HIGHER, STUDY SAYS

As a veteran himself, his interest was piqued. The article focused on a recently completed Texas university study that determined that suicide rates were higher among veterans. He sort of knew that already, because the Post Traumatic Stress Disorder cases from the Gulf War and among veterans of conflicts in Iraq and Afghanistan had caused numerous veterans to take their own lives.

But other deaths from a variety of causes seemed unexplained by the study. These included strokes, heart attacks and pulmonary illnesses, among others. While these occur in the general population, why would they occur more frequently among military veterans and even their family members who had not served in combat situations? The study didn't offer any definitive answers.

He thought again about Marvin Kincaid. No PTSD problems that Marv or Cathy had ever mentioned. Certainly not a suicide. Just a sudden death at a young age. A death that doctors had since called, "Natural Causes," whatever that meant.

Meanwhile, other clients needed his attention. He kept in touch with Cathy and the boys, but couldn't do much to ease their burden, other than financially, since Marv had died.

Autumn was just arriving in Richmond. The leaves were tumbling down everywhere, lending an orange hue and a crisp crackle to the sidewalks along Shockoe Slip. Cooler evenings were already causing diners at The Tobacco Company to bundle up as they left the restaurant or bar. The cooler air carried the inviting smells from the restaurant up, sometimes tantalizing Mike when he sat on his balcony nearby. Less welcome were some of the rowdy, late-night crowds, and occasional altercations, on the side streets as numerous well-lubricated patrons stumbled out.

Tonight, Mike watched the diners scurrying out quickly as they approached the valet parking or zipped around the corner to the public parking garage, their breath already causing little gray puffs of vapor in the cool evening air.

He sat on his balcony, looking across Shockoe Slip to the stately old Berkeley Hotel, slowly puffing on a Carrillo Maduro and sipping a bourbon as a change from his usual Scotch, jiggling the ice and observing the sparse mix tonight of vehicles and pedestrian traffic below. His house phone rang and he went inside to answer it.

"Hi Mike. It's Cathy."

"Hey. How are you and the boys doing?"

"Okay, I guess. They like school and seem to be making some new friends. I called to tell you something I thought you would find interesting."

"Sure, what is it?"

"It took a long time, but I just got Marv's autopsy report."

"Any more specifics about the cause of death?"

"No, not that. It mentions a stroke and heart failure, but no more details. But it's what it doesn't mention that's upsetting me."

"What do you mean?"

"Well, Marv was taking three different prescriptions for his atrial fibrillation and cholesterol. The autopsy report lists only one medication found in his system...the one for cholesterol. It was a statin... one of the common ones you see advertised on t.v. all the time.

I thought he took all of them every day. I guess he wasn't taking them all regularly, but that doesn't seem like Marv. He was pretty regimented. If he wasn't taking all of his meds, especially the two that were supposed to control his atrial fibrillation, I'm really pissed at him!"

"Yeah, that's odd. Well, maybe he just forgot that day. Are you okay?"

"I'm trying to be."

They talked for a few minutes more and when they were finished, Mike felt down. He finished the Evan Williams bourbon, sucked on the ice cubes left in the glass, and sank into the sofa, reaching for the remote for the t.v. After a while, with the help of the bourbon and some boring reporter droning on in the background, he drifted off into an unexpected nap.

BACK IN TOUCH

Mike hadn't met anyone new to date in months. He always ended up thinking about Kimberly eventually, and regretting that while their paths had crossed a few years ago, they seemed to always be separated by so many miles. She was so easy to be around—smiling, intelligent and pretty with her long, light-brown hair, expressive brown eyes and great laugh that he found irresistible. She had an athletic build that showcased her curves. He had noticed that frequently. He loved her quick wit and great sense of humor, too. She was the total package. Right from the start, there was an attraction to her that he had not felt with anyone else.

He decided to give her a call that evening after work.

"Hey, what's up, Doc?"

"That's funny! I think Bugs Bunny has a patent on it, though!"

"How are things in Chicago?"

"Fine. I love my job. I'm already getting to do some research that's pretty exciting.

I'm working on some Parkinson's-related stuff. I'm also finding out how much of a problem counterfeit drugs are. Things like fake Viagra. I had no idea. Our lab has been hired by several large pharmaceutical firms to do research for them related to that. We can analyze medications to break them down into all their chemical properties. Some of the results I've seen are very surprising. There's a lot of bogus stuff circulating out there."

"That's interesting. How's your family?"

"They're all good. Mom's doing a lot of volunteering and dad's immersed in 'Osprey Ongoing Operational Development'...or something."

"Well, it's a really neat aircraft. I never got to fly in one. I was in and out of CH-46s and CH-53's when I was in. I even did some sport skydiving in Okinawa, but just from helicopters. I'd love to fly in an Osprey."

"Yeah, you told me once about the skydiving. Are you crazy?"

"Nah—and statistically, it's safer than a lot of other things. You even have a reserve parachute in case the main one malfunctions. What more can you ask for?"

"Well, I still think you're nuts. I'm glad you aren't doing that anymore. Back to the Osprey--maybe my dad can arrange a ride sometime."

"That would be cool. Hey, listen. I think I can get a few days off around Thanksgiving this year. What would you say to getting together? You can show me around Chicago. I've been there, but really just passing through a few times."

"You know, that sounds like a really great idea! I'll be off, too. In fact, you know my folks would love it if you'd join us for Thanksgiving. But what about your mom?"

"Well, since my dad passed away, my mother likes to spend most of the holidays at her sister's in Delray Beach. Plus, it's warmer down there in November and December. I could go there, but I haven't seen you in ages and really would rather spend some time with you. I'll be seeing my mom at Christmas time, so just a month later."

"I feel the same way. I miss seeing you. Thanksgiving at my parents' would be fun."

"It's not my intent to wheedle my way into a free meal at your parents' house. I just would love to see you."

"Well, I want to see you, too, but trust me, my mom is a much better cook than I am. Believe me… you really don't want me to cook the turkey at my place."

"Well, if I'm invited, I'll certainly accept. Or I'd be glad to take you out to dinner if you prefer to do that. Either way, it would be great to see your folks again. It's been a long time. I'd love to talk with your dad about his last year or two in the Marines, and his new job with Bell-Boeing."

"Okay, let me talk with mom and get back to you, just as a formality. I know they'll want to see you—but as you say, either way, if you don't mind flying out here, we can spend some time together. But there's no way we are eating Thanksgiving dinner in a restaurant! By the way, how is that family doing—the one where the Army friend of yours died?"

"Yeah, doing the best they can, I suppose. It's funny, I just read something recently about military veterans having higher death rates than other people. It makes you wonder if maybe there was something they missed with Marv. He wasn't even 40 yet. On the other hand, I talked with his wife. She got his autopsy report and it seems as though he wasn't taking his medications for his atrial fibrillation."

"Yeah, that's bad. It can generally be pretty well controlled with prescription meds. But who knows? That's awfully young. I feel bad for the family, especially his boys."

"Yeah, me too. So...let me know about Thanksgiving, okay?"

"Okay, will do." After talking a while longer, Mike said goodbye and hung up. The prospect of seeing Kimberly in Chicago was an awesome feeling, and he grinned as he thought about it.

13

Friends in High Places

U.S. Senator Henry Royce had been elected four times by the people of California to serve in the U.S. Senate. He was a powerful member who sat on numerous committees, including the Senate Armed Services Committee, the U.S. Senate Appropriations Subcommittee on Defense, the Senate Committee on Commerce, Science and Transportation and others. He had been instrumental in shaping U.S. policy for more than two decades, especially regarding matters pertaining to the military.

He was especially proud of his record when it came to finding ways to cut the defense budget, which he always felt was bloated. A Democrat, he thought the military spent too much on programs not directly related to defense, such as housing, travel and pay. He preferred to have the federal government spend much more on the social programs his constituents favored, and on the environment and the numerous pet projects his donors wanted him to support. Those things were always on the Democrats' platform.

One of his particular dislikes was the military's 20-year retirement plan, which he considered much too generous at the expense of those social programs, which his wealthier constituents and environmentalists wanted.

Someone could enlist at 18, retire at 38, and receive pay and benefits for another 50 years. That included full medical care and prescription medications not only for the service member, but for their spouses and for their dependent children. That was almost as generous as Royce's own Congressional plan, and he thought himself to be much more important than some chief petty officer or major.

He was getting on in years, but maintained a hectic schedule of committee meetings, sub-committee meetings, Senate meetings and meetings of the full Congress. He had developed an extensive network of contacts throughout the government at the state and federal level and in the business world.

C H A P T E R

14

Mexico

Far to the south, separated from Washington, D.C. by geography, language, culture and international borders, ensconced in a remote part of Mexico, Pablo Vasquez had done his homework. He read the U.S. newspapers and magazines regularly. He scanned on-line news sources including CNN, MSNBC, Fox and others. He probably knew more about the U.S. Congress than most Americans. He studied biographies of the most influential U.S. senators and representatives. This is how he knew how Senator Royce felt about the military. It went beyond antipathy to disdain.

He also knew that Royce liked nice things. The senator had several big homes, expensive cars, staffs of people and a wealthy lifestyle. It wasn't as lavish as Royce wanted it to be, though. A man like this always wanted more, and Vasquez was sure of it. That was how he would tap into Royce's greed.

Vasquez knew Royce would be wary of dealing with him, perhaps even fearing a government "sting" operation. He had to convince Royce that he could make him very rich, and that he really was who he said he was. Most of all, Royce had to feel secure. Vasquez had to meet Royce in person. The time would come. In the meantime, Vasquez waited...and planned.

Weeks passed. It was a fall day when Congress was not in session. The senator was having lunch alone in a small restaurant near his home when Vasquez approached him. While he had an accent, Vasquez spoke English almost fluently and had dressed well in a black business suit with a teal tie and matching handkerchief in his jacket pocket. He looked like a successful, wealthy executive.

"Excuse me, Sir. Aren't you Senator Royce?"

Royce looked up briefly, somewhat annoyed at the encounter.

"I am. I'm not working today though. I'm just enjoying a quiet lunch. What can I do for you?" His tone clearly showed that he didn't want to be bothered.

"Well, I think we can do something for each other, but if you are not interested in earning several million U.S. dollars, I will leave you to your lunch."

Royce was immediately interested, but as anticipated, was nervous about entrapment. Maybe this guy was wearing a wire to record what he said.

"I'm sure I would not be at all interested in your proposal, but thank you anyway."

"Very well, I understand. Sorry to bother you."

Vasquez turned and left the restaurant.

The next day, a package arrived at the senator's home by courier. It was marked "Personal for Senator Henry Royce."

As he opened the envelope, Royce found a DVD and a cell phone. There was no note.

He put the envelope aside, but was intrigued by the contents. After dinner, he helped his wife load the dishwasher. As she settled into her favorite chair with a crossword puzzle, he picked up the envelope.

"Hon, I have some paperwork to do."

"But you're not in session. Can't you just relax tonight?"

"You know how it is. It shouldn't take long. Just a few things I need to look over."

Heading up the ornate staircase to the third of his home's four levels, he closed the door to his home office, which smelled of coffee thanks to the scented candle he liked to burn on the credenza near the window. Warm wood tones and thick, burgundy carpeting gave the large room a regal air.

He settled into his soft, brown tufted leather chair with a squeak and ignoring his government computer, turned on his personal laptop. It whirred for a moment, then lit up. He unfailingly kept it and its contents separate from the other laptop computer he used for official business.

Opening the package, he inserted the DVD into his laptop, setting the cell phone on top of the desk.

As he watched, the disc loaded and presented him with a table of contents.

Listed were:

1. Introduction
2. Statistics
3. Photos
4. Proposal

Clicking on the introduction, he saw a photo of the man who had approached him the day before in the restaurant. Along with the photo was a brief Vitae of the man—a biographical sketch that unabashedly--proudly, really--listed his criminal background, along with copies of newspaper clippings from Mexican, various South American, Central American and U.S. newspapers. Some of the headlines referred to Vasquez by his nickname: El Carnicero—the Butcher.

In section 2, Royce found charts, graphs and narrative descriptions of the size and scope of Vasquez' operation—but carefully constructed so that no details that could be used to locate him or his facilities. Royce found the financial information quite interesting. If true, these drug-related operations had to be staggeringly profitable.

Section 3 showed photos of the interiors of facilities, along with railroad routes, trucking distribution centers and more.

Section 4 was the jewel. In it was a matter-of-fact proposal from Vasquez—work with me and I will make you rich beyond your wildest imagination.

The proposal ended by saying that if Royce were interested, he could use the cell phone to call the private, international number programmed into it to discuss a possible business arrangement.

Vasquez had also included a statement to reassure Royce, saying that while various U.S. and Mexican law-enforcement agencies vigorously pursued illegal narcotics operations, the efforts to combat counterfeiting were puny by comparison.

Vasquez' operations, he explained, focused on counterfeit pharmaceuticals that looked just like the real thing and sometimes (although in truth almost never) even approximated their effectiveness. That last part might give Royce the emotional balm he needed to maybe take the risk and get involved with Vasquez.

Royce scarcely slept that night. Clearly, if what Vasquez sent him was all true, the Mexican had taken a tremendous chance. Royce could turn the DVD over to any of several U.S. investigative agencies, including the D.E.A., the Drug Enforcement Agency.

He tossed and turned and contemplated and imagined. He shifted from thoughts of millions of dollars to thoughts of prison and his reputation and then back to thoughts of millions again. And certainly, the fact that Vasquez was able to enter the United States as though he were just another tourist, rather than the internationally hunted criminal that he was, spoke to his resources and abilities to thwart the law. Maybe he was capable of everything the DVD spelled out. The thoughts of millions ping-ponged through Royce's brain all the next day.

Vasquez' Empire

Pablo Vasquez had ruthlessly murdered his way to a monopoly in the Mexican counterfeit drug realm. He had swallowed up his competitors' factories, vehicles and workers. His largest facility provided security, ground transportation and proximity to rail terminals in several U.S. states, most notably Texas, where his products could be sent on to U.S. distribution centers.

In neighboring Guatemala, Vasquez gradually was gaining the same kind of strength and notoriety among his peers. He knew that in the past three years, more than 1.2 million illegal drugs had been seized by authorities, and that was only a small part of the actual number of counterfeit drugs produced in Guatemala, Honduras and Nicaragua.

In these other Central American nations, as in Mexico, many low-income individuals and families eagerly sought out less expensive options for medications, and businessmen like Vasquez sold them locally for far less than the legitimate brands.

Unlike his operations in Mexico, which only produced counterfeit pills and capsules, a large number of counterfeit medications produced in Guatemala were injectable solutions, including fake versions of various vitamins, pain killers and antibiotics. Cough syrups also comprised a fair percentage of the fake drugs packaged there.

Vasquez, ever the entrepreneur, wanted to expand his business beyond Mexico and into several other Central American countries, and he wanted to include these liquid counterfeit pharmaceuticals in addition to the pill form of the products he was shipping globally.

16

Militaria

Mike had flown in and out of Chicago's O'Hare Airport a few times over the years, mostly to catch connecting flights to other cities. It was always big, boisterous and busy, like the City of Chicago itself. Besides the Chicago-style hotdogs sold there, smothered in pickle relish and onions, one of his favorite things about the airport was the WW II Grumman F6F-Hellcat on display inside one of the terminal buildings.

The Hellcat was the type of aircraft flown by Medal of Honor recipient (not "winner," Mike remembered), Butch O'Hare, for whom the airport was named. The Medal of Honor (MOH)—and NOT "Congressional Medal of Honor," as some mistakenly called it, is not a prize. It is a medal earned in recognition of extraordinary courage in service to the nation in time of war at great personal risk.

Many of the recipients, unlike Corporal Mackie at Drewry's Bluff in 1861, earn the medal "the hard way" – posthumously, as did Lieutenant Commander Edward Henry "Butch" O'Hare on November 26, 1942 in action against Japan.

Mike enjoyed anything that was military or military-related—museums, aircraft, ships, military vehicles, weaponry or whatever. Marine Corps equipment was of course his favorite, but he liked it all.

Various Civil War sites dotted the Richmond area. A few months ago, he had spent a few hours at the Tredegar Ironworks site in Richmond, not far from Belle Isle.

———◊———

Tredegar manufactured cannons and armor plating for Confederate ships during the Civil War. It was a great place to visit and was right next door to a Civil War museum.

Confederate General "Stonewall" Jackson's shrine was just up the road in the Fredericksburg area. It was a farm house where he was taken after being mistakenly shot by one of his own men. He died there and the Confederacy lost one of its great generals.

Mike also had been to the Museum of the Confederacy in Richmond and to the National Museum of the Marine Corps near the Quantico Marine base several times. The latter was one of his favorite ways to spend a day off from time to time.

The exhibits at the Marine museum changed and were updated all the time, but some of the permanent displays always were worth seeing again and again. The museum gift shop was stocked with every kind of Marine memorabilia imaginable, and he always ended up adding to his collection of tee shirts, plaques, bayonet letter openers, mouse pads, shot glasses and whatever else caught his eye. On top of all that, he got to talk with other Marines, both active-duty and no longer serving, which he always enjoyed.

The museum was just about an hour from Richmond—not a bad drive. On the second deck, (or floor, in civilian terminology) the mock-up of Tun Tavern, the Philadelphia birthplace of the Marines in 1775, had the best Black Angus burgers he'd ever tasted-- and Richmond's own Legends craft beer on tap to wash them down. It made him hungry just to think about it.

Today, though, it was turkey that was on his mind—well that, and Kimberly.

17

Chicago, Illinois

Kimberly had offered to pick him up at the airport, but he had decided to rent a car so he could drive around and explore the famous Navy Pier and the rest of Chicago anytime they weren't together. He wanted to at least get a peek at Lake Michigan. He hadn't made hotel reservations, figuring that in a city the size of Chicago, he'd be able to find a room someplace, even during the holidays.

Frankly, he was hoping he might end up staying at Kimberly's apartment. They hadn't talked about it. While they'd never hooked up, they both were a few years older now. The last few times they'd been together, things had heated up between them and it almost happened. He was out of the Corps now and while he had the utmost respect for Kimberly's parents, he didn't have the same outright fear of her father that he had as a lieutenant. He'd play it by ear, he thought, and see how things worked out. But he was a hopeful man.

He picked up a car at Hertz. It was a red Toyota, nice and shiny, with a tan interior. It was a lot smaller and less peppy than his Mercedes, but he thought it would be fine for the few days he'd need it. Pulling out of the airport's auto rental garage, he called Kimberly's cell phone number.

"Hey, are you here?" she said.

"Yeah. It was a good flight...no bumps. Really quick from RIC. So, where am I meeting you?"

"My place. I'll text you the address. It should take you about 25 minutes."

"Excellent! Can't wait to see you."

On the way, he'd stop for some wine—no, Asti Spumante, he thought. It would be appropriate to celebrate Kimberly's recent graduation, new job and new apartment. He also Googled a florist and thought he would bring her a plant as a house-warming gift.

It was a gray day and the famous Chicago winds were blowing. He could hear the breeze whistling over the Toyota as he drove. The city skyline came into view in the distance almost immediately as he drove away from the airport. He remembered one previous visit years ago when he had stayed in Chicago for two days. He had gone up in the Sears tower and still remembered seeing an airplane flying below him. It was probably either leaving or approaching the airport, but it still had seemed unusual to him.

There was no shortage of places to shop between the airport and Kimberly's place. Mike took an exit off the Kennedy Expressway and found a metered parking space. He was lucky—this store had both of the things he wanted, and he was soon on the road again.

To Mike, Chicago always seemed like a miniature rip-off of New York City, right down to the elevated train tracks and subway stations that crisscrossed the city. Trains tagged with graffiti looked just like those in NYC, he thought. He knew Chicago natives wouldn't appreciate those thoughts, so he kept them to himself whenever he met someone from the Windy City.

He drove past tenement buildings and old, brick row houses, although the row houses looked more like those in Philly near the Eagles' stadium than the architecture in parts of the Big Apple, he thought. The trains rattled and creaked above him as pedestrians dodged in and out in front of cars and trucks, daring them to strike, it seemed. Street vendors of all sorts made the interplay of characters and vehicles even more challenging.

Checking the GPS map on his phone, he realized he was getting close to Kimberly's place. Soon, it loomed ahead, a tall, modernistic building, monolithic in appearance, with lots of windows and not much charm. He drove by, looking for a place to park. After a few minutes of searching, he saw someone pull out from a space. He parked on the street and walked the block and a half to the building. The acrid smell of automobile exhaust and bus diesel fumes was strong and irritating.

After riding up on one of the two elevators, which he took because he was carrying flowers and the wine, he walked down the long, carpeted hallway full of green doors and knocked on the one to Kimberly's apartment.

She opened the door, wordlessly throwing her arms up to grab him and pull him in for a long, tight hug. She looked amazing, he thought. There was just something about her...a chemistry they had. She kissed him—three quick times, and then they settled in for a long, passionate kiss that Mike felt literally tingling in his spine. He thought he might drop the bottle, but clutched it hard.

"Well, hi! So far, I like very much your Chicago greeting customs," he said, smiling.

Kimberly danced a small, "happy dance" that made him laugh. She took the house plant and said, "Thanks. Not necessary, but duly noted!"

"You know, I really miss you," Kimberly said, grabbing his hand and leading him to a tan sofa that looked brand new. In fact, all the furniture was new. It was clear that she'd furnished her apartment with a lot of new things, or at least it looked that way to Mike.

Her apartment was on the 9th floor, with a small balcony overlooking the bustling city. It was a nice place, but smaller than his more open-concept loft apartment in Richmond. He definitely preferred the feel of his loft in Shockoe Slip. This was much more contemporary, and he missed the old, worn brick walls inside his apartment.

Still, this was Kimberly's place, and he was here with her. He didn't really care about much else at the moment. He'd thought of her so often.

Even though he'd had fun with Cindy and had enjoyed a couple of other short-term relationships, he had never met anyone who made him feel as comfortable, and yet as excited at the same time, as Kimberly did. Also, there was that unequaled attachment to the Marine Corps that they both shared. They had a history together. That was something nobody else had.

Mike put the Spumante on the coffee table and then eased onto the sofa, and Kimberly sat next to him.

"I'm so glad you came! Thanks for the wine and the plant!"

"Me, too. Let's pop the cork in a bit. It's been too long. Also, I've just lost a good friend and that, along with all the normal stuff, and frankly, still adjusting to being out of the Marines...I admit it's been a lot to deal with. I needed a break, and there's nobody I'd rather be with."

Changing the subject to lighten the mood, Mike looked around the apartment.

"So, all new stuff?"

"Most of it in this room is. I got most of it at one of those places where you buy the whole room full of furniture in one package deal. It's probably not the best quality, but it seems okay and the price was right.

I also have an old bedroom set that was my parents' years ago. The bed is super comfortable. The frame is old, but the mattress is brand new. Want to see it?" She gave him a big smile and tugged on his arm.

"Um, yeah." He didn't want to jump to conclusions, but on a scale of 1-10, Mike's hopes just blasted off to about 5,000.

The bed was a queen-sized poster bed, its dark mahogany wood visibly but somehow nicely scuffed here and there, no doubt from countless moves while the Sheffields traveled the world on orders from the Marine Corps.

Marine families have a saying, "Home is where the Marine Corps sends us." The bed had character. The matching dresser and chest of drawers, a small vanity and stool, and one night stand, rounded out the furniture in the bedroom.

A squat yellow lamp on the nightstand and a combination fan and light ceiling fixture provided more light. There were two small windows, one on each side of the wall where the dresser stood between them. Kimberly had hung her large Temple diploma, framed in gold, on the wall at the foot of the bed. It was the largest diploma he'd ever seen— much larger than his from VCU. Then again, she was technically a "doctor" of pharmacology.

She sat on the edge of the bed and patted the mattress.

"Try it."

Mike sat next to her and bounced lightly.

"It's pretty firm," he said.

"Let's check," Kimberly said, her hand sliding up his leg and lingering there. "Yep, sure is," she said. Kissing him deeply, she asked, "Would you like to do something about that?"

Mike awoke nearly two hours later. Kimberly was still sleeping, nude and wrapped in the comforter, her hair partially covering her face as she lay with an arm outstretched toward him.

"Best Thanksgiving vacation ever!" Mike thought to himself, smiling broadly.

A few minutes later, Kimberly stirred. She grinned at him, but then her facial expression changed quickly.

"Oh, my gosh, I forgot to tell my folks your flight was okay. They'll be concerned. Let me call now…

Wrapping a blanket around herself, she leaned over and took the phone from the nightstand, settling in against pillows she piled up against the bed's headboard. Mike just looked at her admiringly and couldn't believe his luck.

"Hi, mom. Mike's here. His flight was fine. What time should we be there tomorrow?"

"Anytime, honey. We'll be eating around 5, but come early."

"Will do. Can I help you with anything?" No, your dad will be my sous chef, as usual. Just show up with Mike."

"Did dad ask you where Mike was staying?"

"Do you know your father? Of course he did. I told him, 'Don't ask, don't tell,' just like the military says. Don't worry about it."

"Love you, mom!" Kimberly smiled broadly and her gaze met Mike's.

"Love you, too, Sweetie. See you tomorrow."

18

Perks

Like all of his contemporaries in the U.S. Congress, Senator Henry Royce enjoyed a long list of benefits. There was the famed Congressional Cafeteria and its full range of meal choices, and also fitness facilities, numerous extended vacation times and recesses and hefty pensions determined by the members themselves, along with excellent health insurance. In fact, the Federal Employees Health Benefits Program offers many different health care plans. Included are generous prescription drug plans.

Royce was a senior citizen and needed daily blood pressure medication, along with two that he took for high cholesterol. His staff members routinely ran a wide array of errands for the senator, and often, this included picking up prescriptions for him. Like one New York senator who pronounced that "regular" citizens don't need to own firearms, despite the 2nd Amendment's clear directive that "...the right of the people to keep and bear arms... shall not be infringed," Senator Royce had no problem feeling that he deserved all of his medical and prescription drug benefits, despite believing that military service members and their families should not necessarily have equivalent benefits, which he thought were too costly.

So it was that Dan Greenfield, a young Congressional page, was sent to retrieve Senator Royce's prescriptions on this brisk afternoon.

Eager to please and proud to have been chosen (even though his father's numerous D.C. connections made him a shoo-in,) Greenfield looked sharp in his jacket and tie and thought of himself as getting in on the ground floor of his own future Congressional position...hopefully.

Greenfield delivered the medications, and two D.C. newspapers, along with the ***New York Times*** and a copy of **FORBES** to Traci Godfrey, Senator Royce's personal administrative assistant. Nothing got in or out of the senator's office without going through Traci and passing her scrutiny. If anyone knew the inner workings of the senator's day-to-day life, schedule, visitors and more, it was Traci.

19

THANKSGIVING

Kimberly and Mike arrived at the Sheffields' a few minutes early. As Kimberly opened the front door, the aroma of turkey roasting was heavenly. Kimberly's dad had a wood fire going in the living room fireplace—a crackling, aromatic and pleasant counterpoint to the cool Chicago afternoon.

"Happy Thanksgiving, dad!" Kimberly said, rushing to hug her father. Mom was right behind him, and waited her turn to embrace.

"You remember this Jarhead, I'm sure."

The general grasped Mike's hand and pulled him close, roughly but in a way that said, Marine to Marine, that he was truly glad to see him again.

"Hey, Marine!"

"Sir, great to see you and Mrs. Sheffield again! Thanks so much for inviting me."

"Please call me Stephanie," Mrs. Sheffield said. "It's our pleasure, Mike. Kimberly's been excited to have you here in Chicago, and it'll be good for all of us to catch up. Come on in and sit down," the general said.

"What are you drinking these days?" he asked.

———·:·———

"I remember that you like Scotch. I brought you a bottle of a single-malt I like. I hope you like it, too. I'll join you in one if that's okay."

"You bet. Rocks?"

"Yes, Sir."

The general set the bag containing the bottle of Glenfiddich Signature 12 Year Old Speyside on the small bar and took the bottle out. "Ah, good stuff!"

"I've had it before. It's smooth," Mike said.

"Kimberly, how about you?"

"That stuff's too strong for me! White wine would be great, dad, thanks."

The general poured the Scotch and poured wine for the ladies. Everyone sat on the sofas facing the fireplace and drank in the beverages, the smells from the kitchen and the ambience.

Kimberly's brother, Zach, arrived about an hour after she and Mike got to her parents' house. He had driven in from Milwaukee where he worked as a traffic engineer for the city's Transportation Department. Phillip, her younger brother, was away and in school at Duke. He wasn't going to be home for Thanksgiving, but planned to be in Chicago in a few weeks for his winter break.

———·:·———

Dinner soon was ready. The general, Zach, Stephanie, Kimberly and Mike sat around the dining room table and the general led them in saying a blessing before the meal. Mike seized the opportunity to grasp a champagne flute and offer a toast to the host and hostess, and to Kimberly on the occasion of her recent graduation and new job.

"May I offer to General and Mrs. Sheffield, um, Stephanie, my thanks for the invitation and best wishes for health, happiness and prosperity in all you do. Sir, thank you for your service, and may your time with Boeing be everything you want it to be. Kimberly, we all are so proud of you! May your career be rewarding in every way and may you discover a cure for one of mankind's most vexing diseases! Zach, great to see you again!"

"Here, here! and Semper Fi!," the general said.

The turkey was delicious and Mike accepted one of the legs to go along with the white meat he'd been served by Kimberly's mom. Stephanie had made all the traditional sides—mashed potatoes, stuffing, green bean casserole, rolls...there was nothing missing and it was the best meal Mike had enjoyed in a long time, not only because of the food, but because of the family atmosphere he missed.

Everyone had at least a small amount of seconds until they had to surrender and eat no more. It was all delicious and Mike heard himself sigh and wondered if it had been audible to others.

Mike and the general began to help Kimberly with clearing the dishes, but Stephanie intervened.

"Glenn, why don't you guys all go in the living room and catch up? Zach and Mike haven't seen each other in a long time and I know you and Mike must have some Marine Corps stories to swap. Kimberly and I will finish here and we'll have dessert in a little while." Stephanie also wanted time alone with Kimberly to talk about Mike.

"You got it. Come on, guys. Thanks, Steph." The general stirred the fire, added a log, and sat down.

As the men settled in, conversation centered first on Boeing and the general's last command prior to retiring and beginning that second career. It sounded like a great transition and Mike thought Boeing sounded like a good employer. Zach said he was happy with his new career, too. Milwaukee agreed with him and he felt like he had chosen the right career. After a while, Mike shared the details of his accident, recovery and transition to civilian life.

"I hated to get out of the Corps. My back is pretty good most days, but getting hit head-on didn't do me a lot of good. My second career has been going fairly well, but lately, a few things have happened that have been kind of upsetting. I became pretty close friends with one retired Army guy and his family."

———————

"His wife and kids are great and while it started out with me just being their insurance agent, it really turned into a close friendship. The guy—Marv—just died and he was only 39. He's got three boys and his wife really has her hands full. It's a tough situation."

"I remember being on a Pacific cruise and getting a Red Cross telegram, and having to tell one of my Lance Corporals that his young niece had died. It was really tough to be the bearer of such sad news. Now, as an insurance agent, I'm still dealing with loss and the impact on families," Mike said.

"Sorry to hear that, Mike. Lord knows I've lost numerous good friends in the Corps. I also served as a casualty officer for a while when I was a Major. It never gets easier."

After a while, discussion turned to further discussion of Zach's engineering job and the mood got more upbeat.

CHAPTER 20

Departure Day

The sun came up big and bright and as yellow as McDonald's famed golden arches, which Mike could just barely make out down one of the side streets as he looked out from Kimberly's balcony. It had been another romance-filled night and he was really dreading leaving Chicago that evening.

Kimberly returned to the balcony with two coffee refills, her white robe ruffling in the famed Chicago breeze as the coffee aroma likewise wafted with each soft gust.

"Good day for flying...I guess," she said, extending her bottom lip in a dramatic pout.

"Yeah, I know...I really hate to leave. Chicago has been, ahem, very, very good to me!"

"Yeah, well you Richmond boys aren't too bad, either."

He wrapped an arm around her and they stood together, looking out on the constant stream of cars, trucks and motorcycles visible in every direction far below them. Horns blared as the long lines of cars, mostly taxis, seemed to be impatient with everything and everyone. Chicago was a lot busier than Richmond.

Kimberly's cell phone rang in her purse, propped on the arm of the sofa in the living room.

"Hi, dad. What's up? You don't usually call me this time of the day."

———

"Well, I know Mike is flying out this evening, but I thought, if you see him before then, I might get him that ride on an Osprey that you told me he's been wanting. I could arrange it anytime this morning or this afternoon. Why don't you give him a call and see if he's interested?"

"I will! I think he'd love that." It wasn't lost on her that her father, while certainly suspecting that Mike was staying with her, gave her the "out" by suggesting that she "call him."

She hung up the phone and smiled. She was pretty sure her dad knew, or at least suspected, that she didn't need to make that phone call to ask Mike about flying in the Osprey today. "Maybe the old guy is getting soft," she thought.

"Well, that was my dad. Guess what?

"What?"

"Today is your lucky day. Want to take an Osprey ride?"

"It's already been my lucky day—but Hell yeah...when?"

"Anytime, basically. Let's get dressed and I'll call him back. I'm so glad I took the day off to spend it with you...now I can go, too."

"Excellent!"

21

Osprey

Kimberly parked in one of the spaces marked "Visitor" and she and Mike saw an Osprey aircraft sitting on the tarmac beyond the gate at Boeing's Chicago facility. General Sheffield and another man, presumably the pilot, stood near the aircraft, which was painted in patriotic red, white and blue, with V-22 written on the fuselage.

This was one of Boeing's demonstrator Ospreys, used for various displays, air shows and the like. As such, it was "tricked out" with all the options and was a lot "cushier" than the tactical version flown by Marines.

The private security guard at the gate was waiting for them and waved them through and onto the tarmac.

"Dad, this is so neat. Thank you for doing this!"

"My pleasure. Tom is one of our best pilots. He'll be taking all of us up today and will show you what the Osprey can do."

"Hi, Tom. This Marine is really looking forward to the flight," Mike said.

"Glad to have you and Kimberly aboard. Let's get settled."

With everyone buckled in, two crew members took their seats and Tom and the co-pilot, Ryan, started the engines on the Osprey. The rotors were horizontal and the aircraft lifted smoothly off the tarmac and rose to a height of about two hundred feet off the ground.

Tom put the Osprey through a slow, 180-degree turn, hovered for a moment, then turned the rotors vertically and accelerated the aircraft, flying it like a conventional propeller-driven plane. Speaking to everyone aboard on the headsets they all wore, he said, "Okay, hold on. I'm going to take us up quickly."

Pulling back on the controls, the pilot showed off the muscle that the Osprey packed. Everyone, except the general, was amazed and a bit scared by the effect, as their bodies were pressed back into their seats by the force of the acceleration. Just as quickly, Tom transitioned into another hover and the aircraft sat motionless in the air, like a giant humming bird contemplating its next move.

"Wow!" Kimberly shouted.

"Yeah!" said Mike. He was grinning like a Cheshire cat.

Glenn Sheffield just laughed.

Tom flew over a few local landmarks and the co-pilot narrated.

"There's the Navy Pier," he said as the aircraft banked left. The aircraft flew over the Chicago skyline and then out over the water. For about 20 minutes, they studied the inside of the Osprey and listened as Ryan explained a lot more about the aircraft. Everyone agreed that it was a revolutionary design. They looked out over the Chicago skyline and well into the surrounding suburbs.

It was a beautiful day for flying and the large white clouds they flew through from time to time gave the experience an almost mystical effect.

Soon, they approached their departure point and Tom settled the big bird down in a flawless hover finished with a scarcely perceptible touch of the wheels on pavement.

"That was unreal! It's really an impressive aircraft," Mike said when they were clear of the Osprey.

"We think it's special," the general said.

"Dad, thanks so much!" Kimberly hugged her father and then he and Mike shook hands and said goodbye.

Mike and Kimberly left and drove to a coffee shop for a snack and a chance to talk and say farewell as the visit they'd both been anticipating for a long time came to an end. Mike's flight was soon now, and he had to return the rental car and check in at O'Hare.

"This was bad...really bad," Kimberly said.

"What?"

"Spending this time together. I'm going to miss you like crazy now!"

"Believe me, I feel the same way. You're just amazing and your family is so great. But most of all, you're just amazing!" Mike reached for her hand across the table and squeezed it.

"You know we have to see each other again, and soon. How about you come to Richmond next time?"

"It's a deal. Let's talk after you get back home and we can compare our schedules, but I need to see you again real soon. Like real soon!"

Suspicion

Mike twirled a pen in his hand and looked at the screen on his computer. He was spending most of this Thursday in his office, working to come up with some new leads for policies he could sell. He had collected around 40 business cards over the past few months, from people he met socially or through his business dealings. Every once in a while, he would call these contacts to see if they or any of their friends or family might need new or updated life insurance. It was quiet in the office and only phones ringing outside his cubicle now and then distracted him.

He heard a "ding" from his cell phone, which was behind him in his jacket pocket. Picking up the phone, he saw that he had a text message. "Call me tonight," it said. Kimberly had sent it, probably figuring that he might not be able to talk during the work day.

"Roger," he texted back.

The morning passed and he realized he was getting hungry. There was an Italian deli up the street and Mike walked there, grabbed a spot at a small table, and chewed slowly on a sub sandwich. He wondered about Kimberly's text, but since she had asked him to call tonight, he refrained from calling or texting her now. Like him, she no doubt was working today.

⁑

He made a few calls after he got back to his office and was able to set up two appointments, so hopefully it was time well spent.

Back at his apartment after work, he read for a while and then called for delivery from a Chinese restaurant a few blocks away. Richmond offered any kind of cuisine you could imagine, even Caribbean, African, Moroccan…you name it. Tonight, Chinese would do just fine.

Later, he called and heard the phone ring at Kimberly's Chicago apartment. He always had to remind himself about the 1 hour time difference, so he waited until it was 8 p.m. in Richmond to call her.

"Hey!"

"Hey yourself. How are you?" Mike was glad to hear Kimberly's voice and curious to know why she had texted him. Maybe she just missed him.

"I'm okay. Chicago is cold and windy today. Go figure!"

"Richmond's not bad. I walked to lunch today and it was pleasant. I wouldn't mind being in Chicago today, cold and windy or not, if I could see you."

"Sweet. I miss you a lot too. Hey listen, I was thinking about something. Maybe I'm watching too many episodes of NCIS, but remember when you told me that your friend Marv hadn't been taking his prescriptions?"

"Yeah. What about it?"

"Well, people at the lab have been talking more

lately about counterfeit drugs. I've heard about that, of course, as I mentioned to you, but mostly I hear about a case now and then where they find fake Viagra. I didn't really know much about the situation."

"So, what's changed?"

"Not sure, but it seems like it's become a huge problem—like a mega-million dollar problem. I've done some reading over the past couple of days..."

"So...are you saying that maybe Marv wasn't skipping his meds?"

"Well, it's possible, I guess. What if he was taking them, but they were counterfeit pharmaceuticals?"

"No way. His wife told me they got all their prescriptions by mail from the government. I doubt that the U.S. government is selling counterfeit drugs.

"Hmmn. Yeah, that doesn't sound very likely. I just thought maybe there could be something to it, but I guess you're probably right."

"Anyway, it sounds kind of like a matter for the D.E.A or something, not for us."

"It's funny you should say that. If I remember right, my dad has an old Marine friend who is now an F.B.I. big-wig. They were lieutenants together but have stayed in touch all these years. Maybe I'll ask my dad about it and see what he thinks."

"Interesting. Let's think about it and talk more soon."

C H A P T E R

Searching for Answers

little more than a week had gone by since they last spoke. Mike was jogging around Shockoe Bottom after work when his cell phone rang. He glanced at it and saw that it was Kimberly calling.

"Hi. I'm running...let me catch my breath for a minute."

"I can call you later..."

"No..." He slowed to a walk and after a minute, sat on a low fence alongside a parking lot. It seemed like any piece of land in downtown Richmond that didn't have a building on it instead had paid parking areas.

"How are you?"

"I'm good. I wanted to let you know that I spoke with dad and I was right. He has that Marine friend who is pretty senior in the F.B.I. He said he's not sure if it would be D.E.A. or F.B.I. that would be involved with that, but he said he would call him if you wanted to contact him to talk about Marv's Death."

"Nothing to lose, I guess. Maybe he can at least point us in the right direction or let me know if we are wasting our time or just imagining things."

"Okay, I'll text you his name and contact information."

"Thanks. How are you doing?"

"Okay…I think I've mentioned my co-worker, Sue Anderson…she's the one with the daughter who has Cystic Fibrosis."

"Yeah, how's the kid doing?"

"Not well at all, and Sue and her husband are a mess. The thing is that Amy, that's the daughter, was improving on a new medicine for a while. Then, maybe four or five months later, she started going south again."

"So…that's the military family, right? Isn't Sue's husband stationed at Great Lakes?"

"Yeah, that's the thing that has been keeping me up at night. I know we're only talking about two families, but both your friend and my co-worker had a connection to military pharmacies and both had problems that could…or could not, who knows…be related to the prescriptions they received.

"Probably coincidental."

"Mmm, probably. I'm going to poke around a little. I have an idea."

"Uh oh!" Mike laughed. He had learned that Kimberly was very determined when she set her sights on something.

"Well, you know, research is my thing. All those years at Temple and now here at the lab—I'm all about looking for answers."

"Great. Answers is what we need."

⸙

After they chatted a while longer, they said goodbye and agreed to talk again in a few days.

The next morning, Mike called the F.B.I. offices in Quantico, Virginia, and arranged an appointment with General Sheffield's friend, Special Agent-in-Charge Jim Barker.

Back to Quantico

Enlisted Marines talk about being "born" at Marine Corps Recruit Depot, Parris Island, South Carolina or Marine Corps Recruit Depot, San Diego, California. In fact, the Parris Island Marines look down on the "Hollywood Marines" on the west coast in a friendly intra-service rivalry. Parris Island turns out the "real" Marines, they say. In turn, the "Hollywood Marines" think that their mountain marches make tougher Marines. Parris Island is flat and swampy. One thing history has shown to be true...in combat, the enemy can't tell the difference!

In this tradition, Quantico, Virginia, is the birthplace, then, of all U.S. Marine Corps officers. They come there from America's colleges and universities through a number of programs, all leading to Officer Candidate School. All those who make it through that grueling 10-12 week process must pass the rigorous physical, mental and emotional challenges to prove they have the potential to lead those Parris Island and San Diego Marines in combat. While the drop-out rate from the two recruit depots historically is around 15 percent, the drop-out rate at OCS can be 50 or 60 percent or even higher.

———————

After completing college and OCS, young men and women can be commissioned as 2nd lieutenants in the Marines. Some enlisted Marines can earn this opportunity through other programs that allow them to transition from the enlisted ranks to the officer corps. These Marines are known respectfully by their fellow Marines as "Mustangs." The next step in officer training is The Basic School, also located at Quantico.

TBS, as it is generally called, is a more than 6-month-long training program where new lieutenants learn everything they need to know to serve in the Fleet Marine Force. This includes tactics, weapons, naval gunfire and mortar indirect fire plotting, hand-to-hand and pugil stick combat training, topographical mapping and land navigation, first aid, military law and much more.

Mike had all these memories flashing through his mind as he eased Ghost off I-95 at the Triangle, Virginia, exit. He had a thousand memories of those months and of the other men who, like him, had wondered if they had what it takes to be a Marine officer. Somehow, he had made it.

After completing OCS, Mike finished his next two years of college at VCU—Virginia Commonwealth University, in the state capital, Richmond. His shiny gold bars gleaming on his uniform, he proudly accepted his diploma and prepared for the next stage of his life—being a Marine Corps officer.

The next challenge was The Basic School, the crucible that tries and tempers new lieutenants and turns them into leaders in one of the worlds' most fabled and respected military organizations.

Back at Quantico today, he smiled and subconsciously shook his head as he thought about TBS and the captain who had been the staff platoon commander for his platoon there. A bear of a man, Captain Krugg had the build of a pro-football player and the temperament of a wet cat. But, he had been the mentor needed to get his lieutenants through the program.

Mike steered Ghost up to the sentry booth at the front gate to the base. Quantico was the crossroads of the Corps and also was home to the F.B.I. Academy and the F.B.I.'s world-famous laboratory. Today, like most days, was busy at the gate. Two young Marines manned the post. The one stopping incoming vehicles to check driver identification wore a Beretta 9 mm pistol on his hip.

The second sentry carried an M-16 semiautomatic rifle slung over his right shoulder. Both were wearing camouflage utilities—the name Marines use to describe what the army calls BDUs and what many civilians call "fatigues."

Marine terminology is a language all its own. It borrows liberally from the Navy. Marines call walls bulkheads and doors hatches, for instance. Ceilings are overheads and floors are decks.

There are many differences. Some Navy personnel like to remind Marines that they are "part of the Navy." Marines usually reply, "Yes, the MEN'S Department!"

The first sentry greeted Mike.

"Good morning, Sir, what is your destination today?"

"Good morning, corporal. I'm headed for the F.B.I. Laboratory. Can you give me directions?"

"I can, but it's off limits to the public."

"I know. I have an appointment."

"Okay, Sir. They'll check your credentials when you get there. Just go straight and you'll see a sign where the road forks up ahead. You'll want to go right, heading toward The Basic School and the academy. After that, you'll see signs directing you to the academy."

"Thanks."

"The Basic School..." It sounded strange to hear those words spoken. Now that the sentry had reminded him that both TBS and the F.B.I. academy were in the same direction, his memory zipped back to one of the humorous times at TBS.

Captain Krugg had the platoon out on a long march that day. The platoon had their M-16 rifles slung over their right shoulders as the two columns marched side by side. Krugg had alternated lieutenants he selected to call cadence. Some had called out the basic "Left, right, left" occasionally to keep the platoon in step. Others got creative and lifted the mood and the monotony of the march with, "Ain't no use in looking back, Jodie's got your Cadillac. Ain't no use in feeling blue, Jodie's got your girlfriend too! Left, left, your right, left..." Jodie is the mythical guy who steals Marines' girlfriends away from them when they are deployed or in training away from home. Other ditties tended to be more off-color. Marines can swear marvelously, especially around other Marines.

As they marched, the newly minted lieutenants were feeling proud. They sounded good. Their heels struck the pavement in unison and they sounded like a Marine platoon should sound. They reveled in their precision and the platoon had fallen into a nearly trance-like state as they marched, now devoid of any verbal commands. Only the harmonious whack-whack-whack of their boots striking the asphalt was heard.

Suddenly, from the F.B.I. academy on the hill to their left, across from a parked commercial airliner on the right that was apparently used by F.B.I. agents in training exercises, there came a taunting shout.

"Hey, Jarheads! Having a nice walk?"

Captain Krugg heard the F.B.I. agent's comments but ignored them. A small group of F.B.I. agents had heard the platoon and decided to have some fun. It was just a minor interruption to the platoon's marching.

But then, the comments continued.

"Don't you all look pretty!?"

In step alongside them on the left as they marched, Krugg listened to the taunts for a minute and then yelled to the platoon. "Listen up!" He marched them closer to the academy on the hill. "Left, your left, your right..." Just as they got to their closest point to the heckler, now visible on the hill with his contemporaries, Krugg halted the platoon.

"Platoon, halt! Thirty seven pairs of combat boots clicked to a halt with one single sound. "Left, face."

The two columns spun to the left, now facing the heckler.

"Unsling arms!"

"Port, arms!"

"Ready!" Some of the lieutenants were puzzled. This was not standard protocol.

"Aim!" Ah, now Captain Krugg's intentions became crystal clear! Thirty seven M-16s now were leveled at the heckler.

"Now, when I say "Fire," you yell "Bang" as loud as you can!"

"FIRE!"

"BANG!"

Their shout echoed up the hill. Message delivered!

Laughing, they enjoyed a rare moment of levity in their training day.

"Okay, now listen up! Look sharp!" Krugg yelled.

"Order, arms. Port, arms. Right shoulder, arms." Right, face." "Forward, march."

Leaving at least one F.B.I. agent chastened but smiling and 37 Marine lieutenants chuckling, the platoon went on its way. It was a good memory.

Now, Mike passed the golf course, carefully adhering to the 25 mile per hour speed limit. He remembered that there was zero tolerance for speeding on base. He once got stopped for going 3 miles an hour over the posted limit. Then came the brick buildings he so remembered along Quantico's main street. White columns and impeccably manicured lawns showcased the Corps' penchant for discipline and order.

Young men, their heads shaved, walked along the left side of the road, facing him, many carrying their laundry bags. He remembered those days at OCS. Getting out of the barracks to walk into Q-Town, the civilian town of Quantico that was totally surrounded by the Marine base, was a treat for the candidates. It was called liberty. Usually, this was a reward earned late in the OCS schedule.

C H A P T E R

F.B.I.

There it was, the sign the sentry had mentioned.

Ghost turned to the right and Mike drove past a headquarters building flying a red flag with two white stars. A major general was present today on the base. On past a long stretch of nothing but trees, Mike drove, enjoying the sunshine, the memories and the anticipation of meeting Special Agent–in-Charge Barker.

Soon, there was the sign for Lunga Reservoir. He'd marched by that numerous times while at OCS and TBS. Oh, the blisters! Much more fun now, in the comfort of Ghost's leather seats!

A sign for the F.B.I. Academy directed him off to the left, and he could feel his pulse quicken.

Up the hill—THE HILL! He actually heard himself laughing as he remembered the incident with the heckler on this same hill! So much had happened since those days...

"Restricted Area" a large sign warned in big, red letters. "Authorized Personnel Only. Violators Subject to Arrest."

Mike parked the old Mercedes and grabbed his black, leather portfolio out of the back seat. He walked up the shrub-lined walkway into the building and was met by a pretty young woman sitting behind a glass window in the entry foyer.

"Hello, may I help you find someone?"

"Yes, Ma'am, thanks. I'm here to see Mr. Barker."

"Is Special Agent-In-Charge Barker expecting you?"

"He is. My name is Mike DePalma."

"Okay, Sir. If you'll take a seat, I'll see if he is available now."

Mike saw a small waiting area with a few chairs and a sofa. The sofa looked most comfortable, and he sat there, picking up a magazine from the side table. Not surprisingly, it was a law-enforcement publication.

Mike had always felt that the Marines and law-enforcement tended to attract the same kinds of people. In fact, Kimberly's dad had told Kimberly that it was when he was going through TBS that he had met Jim Barker, another Marine lieutenant. They had become friends, and while he had stayed in the Corps, Barker got out after four years and became an F.B.I. agent. They'd stayed in touch, and both had excelled in their respective organizations.

Now, more than 20 years later, Mike was here to see what the general's friend could do to help figure out if maybe someone was responsible for Marv's death, and if so, bring them to justice.

A middle-aged blonde woman in a navy-blue suit greeted Mike in the waiting room. She looked fit and all-business.

"Good afternoon, Mr. DePalma. I'm Special Agent Laskins. Please come with me and I'll take you to SAC Barker. Mike was not sure for a second...oh, Special Agent-In-Charge, SAC.

Mike followed her down a short hall and to Jim Barker's office, where Special Agent Laskins tapped on the door, opened it, and showed him in.

Barker rose to greet him as the door closed behind him, with the female agent following him in and taking a seat in a chair near the door as Barker motioned for him to sit near his desk.

A mixture of F.B.I. certificates and Marine Corps memorabilia adorned the walls of the office. On the leather-covered desktop, Mike noticed a large, wooden cigar humidor. Next to it was an ashtray holding a ceramic cigar that nonetheless, looked quite realistic.

"I'm really glad to finally meet you in person, Sir. I've heard a lot about you. Are you a cigar smoker?"

"God, yes. I started smoking cigars in college and I'm hopelessly hooked on them. Do you smoke them?"

"Every chance I get. I have a catalog from a place called JR's in North Carolina. Have you heard of it?"

"Are you kidding? My car knows its own way there down 95 to Smithfield! I also go to the Havana Cigars shops when I'm in your neck of the woods."

"Wow—small world."

Barker reached into his jacket pocket and pulled out a wrapped cigar.

"I like to try lots of different sticks, but these are my fall-back smokes," he said, holding up an Arturo Fuente cigar. Mike squinted to make out the label.

"Yes, I like those, too. My usual is probably an Upmann, though, or Romeo Y Julieta ," Mike said.

"Also good…"

Cigar talk followed for a few more minutes as

Mike and Barker talked about favorite brands of cigars, accessories and the fact that thawing relations with Cuba might someday mean some more really good smokes being easier to find.

"Well, I'm always glad to meet another Marine, especially any friend of Glenn Sheffield's. And I'm always happy to meet another cigar fan. The S.O.B.s won't let anybody smoke in the buildings here, of course, but we have an outdoor area that I frequent when I can."

Yes, Sir, the general's quite a guy. As for cigars, I love 'em. So we have a couple of things in common—the Marines and stogies." I know that you also served in the Marines, Sir.'

"Please, call me Jim, and Hell yeah, I'm an old Devil Dog."

"Thank you. I really don't know where to start, but I think General Sheffield has told you some of the basics."

"He has, but please start at the beginning for me. Special Agent Barbara Laskins works closely with me and will be sitting in on our conversation."

"Well, as I think you might know, I had to get out of the Corps after a serious automobile accident. I've been seeing Kimberly Sheffield for a long time and recently visited her and her parents in Chicago. I moved back home to Richmond after I got out of the Corps and I'm working for an insurance company.

One of my clients died young and very unexpectedly a few months back, and as things unfolded, Kimberly and I began to wonder if there was something not quite right with some of the prescription medications he was taking—possibly contributing to his death."

"What got you thinking that?"

"It was kind of a chain of events. His death was unexplained. He was a young guy. Then I happened to see a newspaper article that talked about veterans dying off more frequently and younger than the general population. Also, as you might know, Kimberly Sheffield is a pharmacist, and she says her laboratory staff has mentioned an increase in counterfeit or tainted drugs. It all just started to seem that maybe there was something to it. Or it could be nothing at all. Maybe we've been watching too many movies. I don't know."

"It's very possible that there is. Counterfeit drugs are big business, and it's getting worse all the time. Those crimes cross several boundaries in the law enforcement field, but the F.B.I. has been investigating these types of crimes for quite awhile, along with the D.E.A. and a couple of other federal agencies.

When Glenn called me about your interest in this case, I thought we should meet to see if there is anything to your suspicions."

"I don't know how much help I can be with giving you information to go on, but if you think there's enough for the F.B.I. to get involved in looking into it, I'll do whatever I can to share what I know about Marvin Kincaid's situation—that's my client who died. He had atrial fibrillation and was taking a couple of medications that should have kept it under control."

"Okay. Here's my card, with my phone number and email address. Barb will let you have one of her cards as well. You can email either of us any information you have, or anything you come across. Or call either of us. Let's see what we can find out."

"I don't know how to thank you. Marv's family is really suffering, and if counterfeit medications played any part in his death, I'd love to make sure it doesn't happen to anyone else."

"Well, we Marines—and cigar smokers—have to stick together. "Here, try one of these," he said, handing Mike a Gurkha Raptor cigar out of the humidor. "Stay in touch!"

"Thanks! I'll smoke it tonight!"

Mike shook hands with Barker, took a business card from Special Agent Laskins, and followed her down the hall to the entry foyer.

"Thanks again for meeting with me," he said.

"It's our pleasure. I'm sure you'll be hearing from us as the investigation goes forward. Meanwhile, feel free to call me anytime."

"Not bad," Mike thought as he walked away. But Special Agent Laskins was a little too old for him anyway. He smiled.

Mike thanked her, said goodbye to the receptionist and then left the building and fired up Ghost and drove away, feeling optimistic that with the F.B.I.'s resources, if there was anything or anyone to blame for Marv's death, it would become known."

As promised, when he had finished with dinner that evening, Mike retired to his balcony. It was a warm evening, but pleasant. A large, blue and yellow produce truck rumbled down the cobblestones on its way to the Farmers Market in Shockoe Bottom. Something was blooming and there was a fragrance in the air that wasn't unpleasant, although it was accompanied by the yellow menace of pollen so common to Richmond.

Mike hefted the Gurkha Cellar Reserve cigar Special Agent Barker had given him. Mike Googled it. It was wrapped in an 18-year-old Corojo wrapper and at 6 x 58 was a thicker and more solid cigar than what he normally smoked.

At about $14 per stick, it also was way more expensive than what he typically smoked, although he had spent more on occasion when he wanted to splurge or to celebrate something special. He remembered one time in San Diego when he had sat in front of a man-made lake with a large fountain in the middle. Feet propped up on a bench, he had leisurely enjoyed the California weather and a $25 cigar for about an hour. He had wanted to do that at least once...kind of like flying First Class, if only just once. But that kind of indulgence was rare.

This cigar burned slowly and would provide a good hour of unhurried smoking. It was a premium cigar and he appreciated Barker sharing one with him. As he blew wafts of light gray smoke heavenward, he felt his body relax.

C H A P T E R

Discovery

At work in Richmond on a Monday morning a few weeks later, Mike was reviewing a new client's policy. When his cell phone rang, it identified the caller as Cathy Kincaid. Mike picked it up and hoped all was well with her and the boys.

"Hi Cathy, how are you doing?"

"Okay, Mike, thanks. Listen, I was going through some things today and buried in a closet was a small travel bag that Marv had In it, there were two pill bottles. He was taking three prescriptions, but I just found these two. One bottle has just a couple of pills left. The other one has more. I remembered that you once asked me to let you know if I ever came across any of his medications."

"Yes, that's great. I'm glad you remembered to let me know. You know, there's probably nothing to it at all, but my girlfriend (he caught himself saying that) is a pharmacist and was telling me that counterfeit drugs are a growing problem. We both figure it's not likely that the government pharmacy would have any, but it wouldn't hurt to check out Marv's prescriptions just to be sure nothing like that was going on."

"Sure, why not? How about coming over for dinner sometime this week and you can see the boys, pick up the pill bottles and we can catch up on things."

"Love to. What night works for you?"

"How about Friday around 7?"

"Great. See you then." Mike looked forward to seeing Marv's family again.

Mail-Order Meds

athy's house looked good. Someone was cutting the grass and trimming the shrubs. Maybe Cathy was doing it, or the older boys. He hoped that she was getting some help. So sad that it wasn't Marv…Mike took the box of bakery cookies off the front passenger seat. He'd gotten the cookies from the bakery on Cary Street—one of Richmond's artsy areas.

"I hope the boys like these," he thought. The baseball-themed cookies, a bat and ball combination for each of them, should be a "hit," pun intended!

Mike rang the doorbell and Andrew opened the door. His brothers ran up behind him.

"Hi, guys! How are you doing?"

"Hi, Uncle Mike!" Jason yelled from the hallway.

It was good to see them again, but Mike felt a powerful sadness as he realized how much these three would rather be greeting their dad at the door. It just plain sucked.

"Hey Mike," Cathy said, hugging him.

"Hi. Smells good in here."

"Just burgers, fries and carrots. Nothing exciting. Gotta make sure the boys get their veggies along with the stuff they like."

"Hey, I didn't cook it, and it's not at a fast-food place, so it's a winner to me!"

Over dinner, Mike joked with the boys, talked about school and encouraged them to help mom around the house.

"We do!" they assured Mike.

"Sometimes," Cathy smiled. "Why don't you guys go watch some TV while we talk."

"Maybe put your dishes in the sink first," Mike suggested, tousling Jason's hair as he got up from the table. He hoped he had not overstepped his bounds.

They did as he suggested, and Cathy looked forward to some adult conversation as the boys headed into the family room.

"How are you holding up?"

"Aw, Mike, you know. It's tough. I miss him so much. I thought we'd have another 25 or 30 years together. The nights are terrible, and it's overwhelming in a lot of ways. There's the house, the cars, the finances, the kids..."

"I can't even imagine. I'm sure it gets overwhelming to try to handle it all."

"It does. Most of all, I just miss him. Marv really was my best friend, on top of everything else."

"Understood." Mike's lips pressed together as he tried to contain his sadness.

"Let me get those pill bottles, "Cathy said, both to change the mood and to fulfill the reason for Mike's visit.

Mike cleared the remaining dishes as Cathy went to retrieve the bottles.

"Here they are," she said, handing him the two small, brown plastic vials.

Mike read the labels. Besides Marv's name and the prescribing doctor's name, on one there was the medication name and the words, "Generic for Group IV antiarrhythmic."

The label indicated that the medication was issued through the U.S. Government's FASTSCRIPS "Federal Pharmacy Services" mail-order medication program.

Mike shook the bottle gently. As Cathy had indicated, there were just a few pills inside.

The second bottle was an anti-coagulant, also from the government's military pharmacy.

"I see that Marv got these by mail. Did he always get his prescriptions that way?"

"No. In fact, we all used to get our medications from our supermarket. They have a pharmacy there. We used to have the option of using the government's mail-order system or using our own pharmacy.

We preferred picking them up when we were shopping there anyway. But maybe 6 months or so before he died, we were advised that we no longer had that option and we had to get everything through the government's mail-order plan.

While it sounded like a good deal—getting your prescriptions delivered right to your door, we had reservations about it. First of all, Richmond is notorious for having one of the worst postal systems in the country. We always have issues with mail being late or getting lost. We worried about that. We were assured that if that ever happened, there was an override system in place that would let us get them at the pharmacy of our choice.

We still didn't like the whole idea. But, we had no choice. Marv registered and started getting them that way."

"How was it?"

"Not bad, I guess. The medications always came on time, automatically. In fact, Mike was irritated that they always came so fast and accumulated way too much before he needed them. He said the company obviously was looking to charge the government for as much medicine as they could justify. He also fussed about the fact that if a doctor ever changed a patient's medication, they'd have to throw it out, wasting more taxpayer dollars." You know, you can't return any prescriptions."

"Mmmmm. Okay. Well, I'm glad you found these and I'll let you know if it's important. I'm just still curious about whether everything was right for Marv in terms of his medications. I just want to look into it a bit more."

"Thanks, Mike. You're a good friend."

Thanks for dinner. Don't forget the cookies!"

"Yeah, like the boys are going to let that happen!" Cathy smiled.

Mike gave Cathy a quick hug, shook hands with each of the boys, and headed down the steps to the driveway where Ghost was parked.

Somehow, he felt Marv's presence. He hoped Marv somehow knew that he was doing what he could to check in on the family.

The next day, he placed a call to Special Agent-In-Charge Jim Barker. An administrative assistant took a message and said he was in a meeting but would return Mike's call shortly.

About an hour went by, and the phone rang.

"Mike, Jim Barker. Sorry I missed your call."

"No problem. Thanks so much for getting right back to me."

"What's new?"

"Cathy, my client's wife, found two of her husband's prescription bottles that still have pills in them. Kimberly can have them analyzed at the lab where she works, I'm sure, and then I can let you know if there's anything to my theory."

"You could do that, but, why don't you let me have them instead and our lab can do it. That way, we have a better evidentiary chain of custody if we find out that anything criminal in nature is going on."

"Sure. That makes sense. I'll drive them up to you in a day or two."

"Let me save you the trouble and have one of our Agents from the Richmond field office meet you and get them from you."

"Well, sure. Thanks a lot."

"I'll call the Richmond office and they'll contact you tomorrow to arrange a time to get those from you."

"Thanks very much."

"Stay in touch. And Mike…watch your six."

"I will. Thanks again."

Mike wondered why Barker had ended their conversation with the pilots' traditional warning to look behind them for an enemy aircraft.

C H A P T E R

Amy

Kimberly's lab in Chicago was a busy place on this Tuesday morning. The white lab coats whizzed by all day long, as did parcels of all sizes and canisters of various liquids used in testing and formulating medications. One of the white coats slowed and stopped near Kimberly's work station. Sue Anderson had quickly become one of the other pharmaceutical staff members that Kimberly enjoyed working with at the lab.

Unlike Kimberly, who was a certified researcher with a newly minted Ph.D. in pharmacology, Sue was not a pharmacist. Her duties primarily involved shipping and receiving and other inventory-related tasks at the lab.

Sue was older, married to career Navy Master Chief Petty Officer Burt Anderson, assigned to the Great Lakes Naval Training Station. The military family connection drew Sue and Kimberly together and they shared many memories of PCS (Permanent Change of Station) moves, foreign duty stations and all of the other unique aspects of military family life.

Amy, Sue's 13-year-old daughter, had cystic fibrosis, a serious illness requiring frequent doctor's visits, regular medications and careful monitoring. As pharmaceutical professionals, Kimberly and Sue had discussed some of the medications Amy took. They helped a bit, but not as much as anyone would like. A recent experience with a medication seemed promising, but optimism was short-lived.

Now, a drug recently approved by the Food and Drug Administration, Zolcapi, was being hailed by the manufacturer as a true breakthrough medication in the treatment of cystic fibrosis, and Sue expressed that she was eager to get a written prescription for the drug filled for Amy at the Great Lakes Naval Hospital pharmacy. Burt would be picking it up today or tomorrow sometime during the day... most likely on his lunch break.

"We're really hopeful about this." Sue said. Every time a new medication comes on the market, we hope it's going to be the one that really helps Amy. There haven't been too many for her to try."

"I hope this is the one," Kimberly said, squeezing Sue's shoulder.

The rest of the day was the usual mix of routine testing of lab samples, a couple of meetings and a pep talk to all staff from the lab director. Sue left a few minutes early and Kimberly stuck around a little after quitting time. She couldn't help but think about Amy and how excited Sue was about the new medication.

At home that evening, Kimberly did some online research about cystic fibrosis and about some of the older, but still prescribed, medications, as well as about Zolcapi. She learned that Zolcapi was a new combination drug for patients 12 and up and worked by helping substances known as CFTR proteins in the lungs to work more effectively in the body, thereby increasing the quantity and function of other beneficial substances.

It all sounded good and gave Kimberly some cause for optimism. She was eager to discuss what she'd learned with Sue the next day. She also was curious enough to take an additional step. The next day, she contacted the manufacturer of Zolcapi and asked for a sample to be sent to the lab. Such requests were fairly standard by the larger laboratories and drug manufacturers were generally eager for their products to gain more familiarity in the marketplace. Besides, the drugs were legally protected for years before any other company could manufacture generic versions.

"So, did Amy start on the new prescription?" Kimberly asked when she saw Sue in the rest room the next morning.

"Yes, last night. We'll see how she feels in a few days on it," Sue said.

"I looked up some information on it last night and it sounds promising. Let me know."

"I will. Thanks for caring, Kimberly."

"Of course."

Four days had passed when a padded envelope arrived for Kimberly. Inside was a vial containing three Zolcapi tablets.

A few days later, when she had time to spend on it, Kimberly ran some tests on one of the tablets. It tested pure for all of the chemical signatures outlined in the extremely detailed pharmaceutical paperwork that had accompanied the samples.

The next day, she asked Sue if she would take the remaining two tablets for Amy and replace them with two from the base pharmacy.

Sue agreed, and a few days later, Kimberly ran the same tests on those tablets. The results were exactly the same, showing that the Zolcapi from the base pharmacy was pharmaceutically just as it should be. No counterfeit medications there, Kimberly thought.

Over the next month, Sue indicated that Amy was feeling much better on the medication and the family was feeling optimistic that finally a medication was helping Amy.

It wasn't until about four months later, after Amy's prescription had been refilled a couple of times, that Sue came into the lab one day looking upset.

"What's wrong," Kimberly asked.

Oh, we thought Amy was doing better, and she was for a while, but now she seems to be back where she was, just not feeling well at all and having lots of symptoms from her cystic fibrosis, mostly coughing and bronchitis. She has a lot of stomach pain and unusual stools…it's just miserable to see her suffering all the time. We had really gotten our hopes up."

"I'm so sorry," Kimberly said.

Later that night, as Kimberly was at home and reading the latest issue of PEOPLE magazine, she couldn't help feeling bad for Sue and her family. It was too bad that the Zolcapi had not worked out to be an effective treatment.

Over the next few weeks, Sue was increasingly distraught and distracted at work, and it was clear to Kimberly that Amy's condition was wearing on her mother.

"Sue, I'm just wondering about something. Would you be able to bring me one more of Amy's Zolcapi pills? I want to check something.

"Sure, I can do that. You already did that a month or so ago. Do you want to run a different test?"

"No, same thing…just want to have another look."

"Okay." Sue seemed dejected.

The weekend came and went and on Monday, Sue saw Kimberly at the lab.

"Good morning. I have that pill from Amy's prescription."

"Great, thanks." Kimberly took the envelope containing the medication and put it in the pocket of her lab coat.

Nothing more was said about Amy or her condition that day.

On Tuesday evening, after her normal hours at the lab, Kimberly ran the same tests on the Zolcapi sample that she had run a few months earlier on the samples from both the manufacturer and the Great Lakes Hospital pharmacy.

Kimberly knew that nationwide, the Food and Drug Administration testing of new and generic drugs showed that only about 1 percent deviated from acceptable standards. She didn't expect this sample to be an exception.

She tested the pill Sue had just given her using spectrometry, molecule shape analysis and other testing methodologies. For this pill unlike the ones she had tested months earlier, the results were different. The chemical compound proportions were different and the molecular structures were not the same.

This pill was not the pure Zolcapi that Amy had been taking when she was showing improvement of her symptoms. In fact, it contained only trace amounts of some of the drug components, and none of some of the other ingredients. It was little more than a placebo. Kimberly was on to something…but what exactly?

That night, she called Mike.

"Mike, listen, Amy's medicine that came to me from the manufacturer was pure. The pills she got on base for a few months were pure."

"Okay, so no problems there."

<hr>

"Well, not exactly. Amy was doing better on the Zolcapi at first, but now she's sick again and Sue gave me one of the pills Amy got recently. I ran tests on it and the results are not right. It's most likely a fake!"

"So what changed? All of the pills were from the Great Lakes pharmacy, right?"

"Yes, but at first they had to come from the manufacturer because they were new to the market. But after a few months, someone could have had time to counterfeit them and send them to the military pharmacy."

"Yeah, maybe. But that sounds like it would be a pretty major operation. How would they get them into that system? Do you think it really happened that way?"

"I'm starting to think so. Let Jim Barker know."

"I will."

"Everything else okay with you?"

"Yeah, you?"

"Pretty much. I'll call you in a day or two."

"Okay. Miss you!"

"You too. Bye."

THE GIFT

It had been a few weeks since Mike had visited Quantico and met Jim Barker at the F.B.I. Academy. He'd been on the road most of the week and was glad to have a day in the office. At work on this rainy Friday morning, he rolled his chair closer to the desk and reached for the inbox, which held the usual papers pertaining to his various clients. There were policies, riders, correspondence from policy holders and the like. The exception was an 8 x 10," padded envelope that had been delivered by certified mail.

Opening it, he found a silver, bubble-wrapped cigar lighter, handsomely engraved with the Marine Corps emblem on one side and the seal of the Federal Bureau of Investigation on the reverse. The Corps' emblem was scarlet and gold and the F.B.I. seal was red, white and blue.

A note accompanying the lighter read, "Mike, from one cigar smoking Marine to another, I thought you might enjoy this. It's wind-proof and refillable with butane. Hope you like it. Semper Fi, Jim."

Smiling, Mike tried the lighter, which had an adjustable double flame specially designed for cigar and pipe smokers. He was surprised by Jim Barker's generosity. Pocketing the lighter, he was eager to use it soon.

It was a full day of office work—a break from being on the road visiting clients. Instead, he made phone calls to several of them, following up on earlier conversations or checking in with some he had not heard from in a while to see if new births, marriages, divorces or other life changes had occurred. When they did, it presented opportunities for Mike to talk about the importance of updating policies or signing up for new ones.

At home that evening, after preparing and quickly downing a dinner of frozen fish filets, French fries and sliced tomatoes, Mike unwrapped an H. Upmann Original Churchill cigar and settled into his favorite living room chair. He clipped the tip off the cigar with a guillotine cutter and flicked the new lighter he received from Barker, slowly rolling the cigar around as the flame engulfed the tip, giving it a bright, red hue as he puffed. The lighter was an instant new favorite. The Upmann, meanwhile, was one of his old favorites, and Mike enjoyed the mild aroma and smooth draw as he scanned his tablet for the day's news, features and his Facebook page.

Putting his tablet aside, he poked his head outside to sniff the evening air from the balcony, and determining that it was pleasant enough outside for him to find the latest edition of ***Cigar Aficianado*** magazine and peruse it al fresco, he thumbed through the articles and put asterisks next to some of the highlighted cigars he wanted to try on his next trip to a cigar store. Before he knew it, he had finished the Upmann.

Aficianado listed cigars from Nicaragua, Honduras, the Bahamas, the Dominican Republic and other major cigar-producing countries and rated them on a point scale.

Much as wine connoisseurs base their selections on descriptive ratings by wine experts, serious cigar smokers count on ratings and descriptions such as those in *Aficianado* and other publications to help them purchase cigars they will enjoy.

In this edition, there were a couple of cigars rated as high as 94 on a 100 point scale. "Encased in a textually lovely, medium-brown wrapper, this cigar teases the palate with notes of earth and leather with a mildly spicy core and a touch of cherry and chocolate on the finish," read one description.

As was his usual practice, Mike took out his cell phone and wrote down the names of several of the cigars he wanted to try. On his next trip to a cigar store he would bring up the list and buy a few, along with humidor humidifier packets and any other items he needed.

CHAPTER

TO THE LAB

As Jim Barker had arranged, the Richmond F.B.I. field office contacted Mike and an agent met him for lunch at a restaurant where Mike went from time to time. The agent had Mike sign some paperwork about a chain of custody for the two prescription bottles Cathy had given him.

Kimberly said, as Mike thought she might, that she could have had the bottles examined too, but she understood the advantages to having the F.B.I. lab conduct an analysis of the two prescriptions, in case some type of crime was involved, although neither of them yet had any real proof that might be the case.

Meanwhile, still perplexed by the results of her testing of Amy Anderson's Zolcapi prescriptions and the differences in the lab results of samples taken over the past few months, Kimberly had submitted a Freedom of Information Act request to the F.D.A., inquiring about the manufacturer, the production facilities, shipping and other information, especially relevant to shipments of the drug to military facilities, particularly Great Lakes Naval Hospital.

What she got back was heavily redacted, with information that fell under various F.O.I.A. exemptions blacked out. But she did learn that the drug traveled by rail at least part of the way as it transited from the manufacturer to Chicago. That led her to draft another detailed F.O.I.A. request seeking greater detail about American Pacific Railroads' operations. It was listed as having transported the medication.

Since commercial operations are not subject to the F.O.I.A., she limited her request to information pertaining to shipments of pharmaceuticals by the railroad to U.S. military installations, including Great Lakes.

Mike let Jim Barker know about the Zolcapi test discrepancies and Barker said he would have one of his lab technicians contact Kimberly to discuss the tests she had run and have her share the results with the F.B.I.

More Research

Kimberly looked like the stereotypical pharmacist. Her white lab coat was crisply starched and her name tag hung loosely above the pocket over her left breast, the word "Pharmacist" embroidered in blue thread beneath the tag. Similarly clad men and women came and went through the large, stainless-steel and tile laboratory, its bottles, vials and tubes glistening in the afternoon sun streaming through the skylight.

Most of the workers were researchers, as Kimberly was. Others were quality control technicians, with a few computer geeks also on hand to deal with the inevitable computer glitches inherent in a high-tech office.

Kimberly had been assigned to a project team working to verify the efficacy of a new class of drugs for potential use in the treatment of Parkinson's Disease. The drugs showed promise, but the Food and Drug Administration was working with several research firms across the country to determine optimum dosage levels, potential side effects and other vital information prior to approval and full-scale marketing.

On her own time, at lunch or working late into the evenings, and using her professional knowledge to formulate the right wording, she had submitted several more Freedom of Information Act requests over the past few months to various agencies of the federal government regarding U.S. government seizures of counterfeit pharmaceuticals, military contracts for medicines, military installations with hospitals, clinics and any other pharmacy facilities, etc.

She had quickly discovered, after several unsatisfying responses from government agencies, that if you didn't ask for documents in precisely the right way, you would be told there was an exemption preventing their release.

Her professional expertise allowed her to obtain numerous documents others would have most likely not received, and she shared all of them with Mike by email as both of them continued looking into Marv's death. Mike also shared everything with Jim Barker to keep the F.B.I. informed about what Kimberly learned.

She never knew that counterfeit drugs of all types were such big business, not only in the U.S., but in most of the developed countries. She had read a few articles about counterfeit pharmaceuticals at Temple, but now that she was actively working in the career field, she was learning much more about it.

Pharmaceutical research was expensive and time consuming—and fraught with legal implications of all types, especially as relates to any potential side effects. The resultant high cost of new medications, in particular, gave rise to Black Market deals and to incentivizing counterfeit manufacture.

C H A P T E R

HITTING A NERVE

It was a long day. Mike had started out in the office but then was on the road most of the day visiting clients in Richmond, Chesterfield County, Mechanicsville and finally in Williamsburg. Lunch didn't happen. Dinner was a fast-food burger and Diet Coke while he sat in Ghost and looked over paperwork for one more policy he would be working on later tonight at home in order to be ready for an early office appointment tomorrow.

It was nearly 6:30 and he still had about an hour drive home. Tossing the burger wrapper in the bag it came in, he dabbed at the ketchup on his chin and wiped the leather seat where he'd managed to ooze some burger grease.

As he put Ghost in gear to pull out of the parking lot, his cell phone made the cricket noise he'd selected for the ringer.

"Hey!"

"Oh, Mike! This is getting really weird now!"

He sensed something in Kimberly's frantic voice. Was it anger, fear?

"What's going on?"

"I got home about half an hour ago and my apartment has been totally ransacked. I called the police. They're sending a forensics team to dust for fingerprints and I have to try to figure out if anything is missing. It's such a mess!"

"You have to be kidding me. How did they get in?"

"Looks like they might have had a key somehow, because the door and the lock seem like they're not damaged."

"That's spooky. Obviously, once you take a look and see if anything's missing, you need to go stay with your parents until police investigate."

"For sure. I'm not staying here!"

"See if your dad can come and meet you to take you over there. I'd rather you not be alone at all. Or else, leave with a cop until you get to your car."

"I will. I have to go now, the police are here. I'll call you tonight."

"Okay. So sorry about this. It's such a violation and it's unnerving."

"Yeah. And it's scary."

"I know. I'm so sorry. Be careful. Call me later. Love ya."

"Thanks, Mike. You too."

The ride home on I-64 West was quiet...not much traffic at this time of the evening. Mike drove on, preoccupied, not able to shake off the anger and concern he felt from Kimberly's call. He worried about her and was eager to hear what the police had to say once they checked it out.

Soon, the lights of the city rose up from the asphalt and he neared his exit. Ghost slipped into the parking garage and eased into the space. Mike grabbed his portfolio and coffee cup and headed down the stairs from the parking deck to ground level and then around the corner onto Cary Street and Shockoe Slip.

He got his mail from the locked box in the lobby and then ran up the short flight of steps to his loft apartment. Still thinking about Kimberly, he was stunned by what he saw when he opened the door. Piles of clothing, books, pillows and furniture lay everywhere. Broken glasses, mugs and lamps littered the floors. In the bedroom, his computer desk was lying on its side, and his laptop was nowhere to be found.

Everything—virtually everything—was in complete disarray. Even the mattress and box spring on his bed were standing upright against one wall, as if someone had thought he hid his money under them. The mattress and box spring both had been slit open from top to bottom and stuffing material and foam were ripped out in chunks.

"Holy shit!" he muttered.

He reached for his cell phone and pushed the number in memory.

Kimberly answered.

"Oh my God, Kimberly! You aren't going to believe this!"

"What? What's wrong?"

"They hit my place, too. Total wreck in my apartment—everything's broken, tossed around... my computer's been stolen..."

"Mine, too."

"Okay, that's interesting. I haven't called the police yet. I'll do that now and we can talk later."

"I think you should call dad's F.B.I. friend, too!"

"You're right. I think we've hit a nerve with someone, obviously. I'll talk with you later tonight and I'll call Jim Barker in the morning.'

"Sorry, Mike."

"I know...you too! This really sucks. Talk with you soon..."

Mike next called Richmond 911 and the police sent an investigator and a uniformed officer. The investigator called for a photographer and other forensics team members. By the time they finished dusting for prints, taking photos and interviewing Mike, it was after 10 p.m.

He was exhausted now, and deeply worried about Kimberly's news about her apartment as well as what was done to his. Tomorrow, he'd notify his company's homeowners' insurance section about the incident, and once he could put a price tag on the damages, he'd file a claim. He never thought he'd be a customer of his own company.

But now, the question was who had a reason to break into Kimberly's apartment and his home, in two different cities, on the same night? What were they looking for? Why did they take his computer... and hers?

He cleared a spot in the living room and grabbed some blankets and a pillow from the bedroom. He'd sleep on the sofa tonight. Like Kimberly, he found the door and lock to be fine.

He locked the door, checked the sliding glass door to the balcony, and then propped a chair against the doorknob on the door to the condo. He thought he'd get Bill Wilford to change the lock tomorrow. Bill did small jobs like that besides plumbing. Then, sadly, Mike remembered. Bill was gone. Instead, he would have to get a locksmith to change that door's lock tomorrow.

He found a half-empty bottle of Evan Williams bourbon, got some ice cubes and one of the glasses that wasn't broken in the kitchen. He settled on the sofa and after a while, dialed Kimberly again.

"Hi."

"How are you, Mike?"

"Shocked, and royally pissed off, like you. I was floored by your news and I thought maybe it was just a random burglary, but obviously, that's not the case. You and I have rattled somebody's cage!"

"Clearly. What do you think they were looking for?"

"Beats me, but both of our computers are gone, and no other electronics are missing here, as far as I can tell."

"Yeah, as I said, mine is missing, too. I keep a back up of everything on my computer on the cloud, so I ought to be able to get all my files back once I get a new laptop," Kimberly said. I had scanned all the FOIA requests and responses and all the documents I received. Those are all on the cloud. There's quite a lot."

"Oh, that's good. I have some of my stuff on a flash drive on my key ring, too."

"Where are you staying tonight?"

"Here. I propped a chair against the door. The lock is still okay and I have a deadbolt lock that locks from the inside, along with the regular lock. I'll be fine."

"Yeah, well, be careful!"

"I will. I doubt they'll be back. I think whoever did this to us wanted information, not us."

"Okay. I'll call you in the morning. Mike...I love you. Please be careful."

"I promise. You do the same."

C H A P T E R

More Damage

The morning sun danced across Mike's face on the sofa, streaming in from the balcony doors. A crow was being obnoxious outside, doing its best rooster wake-up-call impression. Picking his way through the piles and being wary of broken glass, he made his way to the bathroom. The smell of spilled pine cleaner wafted up from the floor. He had hoped he was dreaming, but this was real. He had hardly slept, turning everything over in his mind repeatedly.

He made a cup of coffee in the Keurig after picking it out of the sink and plugging it in. K cups of coffee were scattered. Making any kind of breakfast was like a treasure hunt. Glass crunched noisily under his shoes, which he'd thought to slip on just in case. Good thing he did. A large shard of glass imbedded itself in the sole of his left shoe.

Sipping on the coffee-black, which was unusual for him, he looked at the kitchen clock. It was too early to call Special Agent-in-Charge Barker, but he would do that soon. Barker would want to know that both Kimberly and he had been ransacked on the same day, in two different states. That took organization and resources—something the F.B.I. would want to know about. It also meant that they were on to something regarding counterfeit medicines.

Scrounging around the condo to find clothes, an iron, a tie, the shoes he'd worn yesterday...everything was so scattered...Mike managed to put together a decent-looking outfit for the office.

Locking the door, he headed for the parking garage. This was interesting...he thought he'd locked the car...

"Crap!"

The car was ransacked, too, during the night. Someone had opened the glove compartment and console, pulled stuff from under the seats...another ransacking. There wasn't anything of interest there, he knew, and the trunk was just about empty except for the spare, jack and some jumper cables. Those were all still there. Whoever had gone through the two apartments, and Ghost, were clearly pros and this kind of thing. Locks didn't stop them at all. But what were they looking for?

Mike got to the office and told his boss what had happened. Next, he called the Richmond Police and left a message for the detective, telling him about Ghost being raided, too.

He called the insurance company's homeowner's group to give them an initial report until he was able to inventory his place for any missing items besides the computer.

Now it was time to call Barker yet again.

"F.B.I. Quantico, this is Libby, may I help you?"

"Yes, Ma'am. This is Mike DePalma calling. Would you please leave a brief message for SAC Barker and ask him to return my call when he can?"

"Very well, I'll give him the message."

"Thanks."

About an hour later, Special Agent-in-Charge Barker returned his call.

"Hi, Mike. What's up?"

"I thought you'd want to know that both Kimberly's apartment in Chicago and my place in Richmond were ransacked yesterday—and also my car was gone through last night."

"Both on the same day, huh?"

"Yes, I thought that was interesting. At first, I thought Kimberly just was burglarized. You know how Chicago can be. But, I don't think this is a coincidence."

"No, neither do I. You both reported the break-ins to the police, I'm sure."

"Yes. Still don't know for sure what's missing, but they took both of our computers. Kimberly has all her files on the cloud. I have most of mine on a flash drive."

"Okay. I'll get both of the police reports. Let me know if anything else develops."

CHAPTER 34

The Deal

The black Cadillac Escalade wove its way down the road, led by a sedan carrying four heavily armed men and followed by another sedan carrying three more. Inside the Escalade, Pablo Vasquez leaned back and immensely enjoyed the undivided sexual attention of a beautiful young woman in the back seat with him as the driver pretended to be unaware of what was happening.

A phone rang and Vasquez knew immediately who was calling. The private number belonged to Senator Henry Royce.

"Esperes! Wait," he said to the woman, pushing her away.

"Hello, senator."

"I...wanted to get back to you. I received the package you had delivered to me and it was very interesting."

"Look, senator, you don't have to talk around anything. Nobody else has this number and nobody knows the number of the phone you are using. It's our private line. It is secure. Relax. Now, are you interested in doing business with me?"

Royce took a deep breath and exhaled. "What can I do?"

"Simple. All I need you to do is to be sure that certain drug shipments headed for U.S. military bases and to the national mail-order pharmacy center for the military are sent to particular railroad stations that I designate. They travel by rail for the major part of their journey, and then by truck. I want you to make sure that the rail part of the trip goes on the routes that I specify. That's all."

"That's all?"

"Yes. We will simply be taking those shipments and substituting exact duplicates. I then keep the originals and the substitutes go on their way for delivery."

"So...what's in the substitute shipments?"

"Nothing anyone will know about. They are just cheaper to make, but they look the same."

Royce thought for a moment. The realization was not lost on him, nor were the ramifications. With counterfeit medications, some military personnel and their families would be getting sub-standard products. But in return, if he could arrange it, he'd get paid a lot of money. But now, he had to figure out how he could influence the delivery locations.

"Give me some time to think about it."

"Don't think too long. The offer has a deadline of 48 hours. And oh, it pays well. I will wire $50,000 to the account of your choice for every month that the shipments arrive at the designated stations. Easy money. Two days. Adios."

The line went dead and Senator Henry Royce gazed at the fountain in his backyard.

"Two days," he repeated to himself, thinking about more than a half million dollars per year in tax-free income.

F.B.I. Interest Heightened

Lunch with a client took Mike to Hondo's steakhouse, off Broad Street in Richmond. He hadn't been there in a while but the mahogany wood throughout the restaurant, the quiet atmosphere and the great service made it the kind of place where you could enjoy the surroundings and talk without having distractions. It was a place he invited clients to if they lived or worked in the area. That stretch of Broad Street, not far from the Short Pump mall and scores of other shops, was a busy place. Hondo's was an oasis of quiet. The food was always good, too.

He sold another policy to Fred Jacobson. This one was for his wife and would bring Mike a nice commission. Driving away after the meeting, Mike decided to stop at the Havana Connections cigar shop, in a strip mall just down the street. He needed to pick up a couple of cigars and wanted to try a few that were highly rated in the latest edition of **Cigar Aficionado** magazine.

As usual, he scouted out the robustos first. He'd found that he usually had just enough time to enjoy a cigar that size. Churchills and the like were for longer periods of relaxation and conversation. Today, he wanted to check out a few brands he had not yet tried. The Nicaraguan Las Calaveras Edicion Limitada 2016 was high on his list.

Aficionado listed it as having hazelnut and roasted coffee impressions with a black cherry and vanilla bean finish. It sounded delicious. Another one was a Honduran Hoyo De Monterrey Excalibur with "gingerbread and candied orange peel flavors." How could he go wrong?

They had the Honduran cigar but not the other one. He bought the Excalibur and three others—two Dominicans and another Nicaraguan—the Villiger San'Doro Colorado Robusto. It had a score of 91 in the magazine, so it should be excellent.

Time now to pick up Route 288 North and head back to his office. Once he got there, he did the necessary paperwork and computer input for Fred's new policy, made a couple of phone calls to keep in touch with other clients, and realized it was almost time to call it a day. He scanned his personal email account and there was a message from Special Agent Laskins, from the F.B.I.

"Please give Director Barker a call when you can. He has some information he wants to share with you. –Barbara Laskins."

On the way home, Mike made the call. Rush hour in Richmond was in full swing and he was glad he had a hands-free feature on his phone so he could stay better focused on the ever changing, bobbing and weaving lanes of traffic. Ghost's powerful engine and maneuverability made the drive as pleasant as possible.

"Hi Mike. Thanks for calling me. Did Barbara tell you anything about what we've learned in the past couple of days?"

"No, Sir. She just told me to give you a call."

"Okay. Well, we've been working with the D.E.A., I.C.E. and other agencies. We're all pretty sure that something is going on involving counterfeit medications getting into the military's pharmacy system, but we're not sure yet how or where it's happening.

"So…maybe my client's medications were bogus?"

"Well, I don't have the lab results back yet from the pills you got from his wife, but it seems that might be a good possibility. Kimberly's tests on the drug her co-worker's daughter is taking sure seem to point in that direction. My technician, Steve Barfield, briefed me after he and Kimberly spoke recently and he says there's no doubt that the later prescription refills the kid got were fakes."

"Hmmm. That could explain something. His wife swears Marvin Kincaid took his prescription medications on time, but on the day he died, not all of them showed up in the autopsy blood work. Maybe what he took were really fakes."

"It's a good bet, Mike. We still have a lot of investigating to do that might lead us to an answer."

C H A P T E R

I.C.E.

Larry Hendrick had been working for Immigration and Customs Enforcement for 17 years. He had worked his way up to a supervisory level and because of his expertise in logistics, he specialized in doing investigative work. One of the things he did was to monitor major transportation companies' routes and activities—everything from Greyhound and Trailways buses, to railroads, to trucking companies and port operators.

Larry knew what moved around the Continental U.S., how it moved, when it moved and why it moved. He had helped I.C.E. to develop computerized systems that provided vast amounts of information at a touch.

The algorithms he'd developed showed Larry when things changed or when the pace of movement varied in a given geographical zone, passenger or cargo category. Over the past six months or so, he'd been looking at American Pacific Railroad with a lot more scrutiny. Some of the algorithms that popped up just looked a bit out of the ordinary. Routes changed, passenger counts changed and deliveries seemed to move at an unusual pace as shipments destined for one port ended up being shifted to another unexpectedly.

Maybe nothing shady was happening, but working with several other federal agencies, including the Drug Enforcement Agency, Larry had homed in on a few things that enabled I.C.E. to get a law-and-order judge to allow a couple of wiretaps. The main concern at this point was human trafficking, rather than drugs.

One of the individuals whose phone was being monitored was the number three guy at American Pacific Railroad, Mark Robbins, who controlled what was picked up, what was delivered, and where.

Several Hispanic women who had escaped from the Mexican coyotes—the men who helped to smuggle them and others into the U.S. through Texas, California and Arizona, told stories of hearing the coyotes and others involved in their transportation speak about a very senior American railroad employee who was involved in sex trafficking of young women from Guatemala, El Salvador, Honduras and Mexico, using his railroad to surreptitiously transport these victims, often without them understanding where they were going or for what purpose.

He facilitated ticketing and transportation for these women, and also apparently for some men who were lured into the U.S. with job offers, only to end up having to perform forced labor. These were contemporary examples of kidnapping and even slavery.

American Pacific Railroad was the most likely railroad to be involved with human trafficking, if there was any truth to these tales. Because of its routes and because he would be the one most likely to be involved or at least aware of these transports, Mark Robbins' phone was being monitored by the feds.

37

Riding the Rails

From Chicago, west to San Francisco...from Minneapolis south to San Antonio and down to the Gulf of Mexico at Houston and to Brownsville, Laredo and Eagle Pass, southwest of San Antonio on the Mexican Border, crossing the vast majority of the Continental United States, American Pacific Railroad weaves a logistics web extending thousands of miles. It carries millions of dollars of freight daily, connecting U.S. cities, and even linking with Canada to the far northwest.

While the trucking industry ultimately delivers goods to local stores and processing plants—everything from clothing, furniture, electronics and processed foods to livestock, it is the railroads that carry those things from the various ports to warehouses and distribution centers—the hubs where truckers can pick them up for further transport.

For international products, barges bring in automobiles and a dizzying array of other items to U.S. ports, where both railroads and trucks converge to transport them to points of sale. At the ports, railroad cars are loaded again in a never-ending cycle.

Along with the staggering amount of legitimate material riding along the web of steel railroad tracks to sustain the needs and wants of a nation of 300 million people are billions of dollars of counterfeit products each year. These range from tee shirts and running shoes emblazoned with name brand logos, to convincing fakes of high-end purses, shoes and other leather goods.

———·✻·———

Law-enforcement agencies make cursory arrests here and there at flea markets and back-alley shops of individuals selling knock-off apparel and accessories, and occasionally are able to temporarily shut down larger-scale counterfeiting operations, which mainly import their wares from various Asian countries.

U.S Immigration and Customs Enforcement, commonly referred to as I.C.E., deals with more than the challenge of illegal immigrants pouring into the southern United States from Mexico. I.C.E. agents also enforce what are often mistakenly viewed as laws that have victimless activities associated with them.

The person buying a fake NFL jersey might not think about the fact that a young child in Southeast Asia worked in a sweatshop to create it, or that someone holding patents, copyrights and trademarks is a real victim of counterfeiting.

The volume of counterfeit materials continues to grow exponentially, and the level of sophistication in producing difficult-to-detect frauds improves incrementally. Many a fashionable lady is ambling through town proudly carrying her Gucci, Coach or Michael Kors purse, never knowing that she paid for an original, but got a well-made, convincing fake.

It is when counterfeiting turns from fashion to pharmaceuticals that the stakes are raised for the manufacturer, the distributor, the seller and ultimately, the user. The results can be disappointing, such as when a counterfeit blue pill fails to produce the desired results in an amorous male.

But while up to 80 percent of counterfeit pharmaceuticals have been of the "lifestyle" type, such as the erectile dysfunction drug Viagra, some counterfeiters have realized the huge, international market for counterfeiting other legitimate U.S.-made drugs as well.

Therein was the opportunity seized upon by Pablo "El Carnicero" Vasquez. Forty six years old, highly intelligent and with a middleweight fighter's build and handsome face, Vazquez had risen through the ranks to the top of a regional Mexican gang. It was not those attributes, however, that had earned him the nickname "El Carnicero," "The Butcher."

In numerous incidents of inter-gang rivalry that had escalated into violence, Vasquez had shown a spectacularly violent pattern of ruthlessly maiming and killing those who opposed the interests of his gang members and himself. He ruled by fear and sheer, sadistic, hyperbolic brutality.

He was creative, often personally killing with knives, guns, acid, clubs, machetes and anything else at hand. Even among the murderous groups of men who knew him, El Carnicero was respected and feared.

Vasquez had been involved for years with trafficking in narcotics. Some had been sold and used in Mexico and Central America, but mostly had gone north to the U.S. across its porous border and south to Brazil and other South American markets.

Law-enforcement agencies had been making progress in fighting the narcotics trade, making many arrests and seizing and destroying large quantities of the drugs. It was getting increasingly more difficult for narcotics traffickers to operate, and Vasquez, along with many others, was feeling the heat.

What differentiated him from most was that Vasquez was really smart. He had a knack for organization and planning, and he thought, and acted, on a grand scale. Using profits acquired over years plying narcotics, he had built a complex network of factories, had hired chemists, engineers, printers and other specialists, and was now operating a drug counterfeiting operation with global reach. His net worth was in the hundreds of millions, but like Senator Royce, he wanted more.

He had lately begun shifting his emphasis to counterfeiting pharmaceuticals, and those included the lifestyle drugs like Viagra and Cialis. But he was growing way beyond those. His business was booming, and expanding. He had hundreds of employees. Best of all, he had a few allies in the U.S. that were literally worth their weight in gold.

C H A P T E R

Congressional Influence

During his long years in the Senate, Henry Royce had made his share of enemies. He had jousted with his peers, both publicly and privately, over policy issues, protocols and appointments. He had been faithful to his Democrat party and was a stalwart protector of his state's economic interests, above those of the nation as a whole. Often, that rankled others.

He also had a lot of friends—fellow senators, congressmen, industrialists and a host of others, each with their own spheres of influence. Influence peddling was how things got done in Washington—good things and bad things, and Royce was a master at it.

Now, he needed to make things happen—good things for him, bad things for the military community.

"Mark, Henry Royce. How are you these days?"

"Good, good. Nice to hear from you, senator," said Mark Robbins, American Pacific Railroad's Deputy Chief Operating Officer, and third in the company's hierarchy.

Some small talk ensued before Royce got to the topic he really wanted to discuss.

"Listen, I have some manufacturing constituents who are trying to save some money on follow-on transportation of shipments. In particular, there are a few of your railroad complexes where they prefer to have their goods sent so they can consolidate that follow-on transportation. This would be a change in some cases from where they are going now.

The thing is, these changes need to be made without any fanfare and rerouting needs to be done automatically, like forwarding mail. There is a need for some, uh, discretion in that the shipments need to be rerouted without the senders or some other parties being aware or involved in the changes.

Is there a way that I could provide you with a list of shipments, say, each month, and ensure that the shipments go only to the stations on the list, despite what the original shipping destination might be? At the same time, some, um, 'employees' will substitute duplicates to go to the originally intended destinations. Just call it selective rerouting."

Robbins paused. It was clear that Royce had a backroom deal going on...probably one that at least skirted the law, if not worse. He knew the senator had a lot of clout in D.C.—clout he needed from time to time regarding railroad easements, new routes, noise complaints and more. He knew that the senator had influence with the Department of Transportation, and that he served on the U.S. Senate Committee on Commerce, Science & Transportation, along with other committees that had the ability to facilitate legislation favorable to American Pacific, or to draft legislation that could be highly damaging to the industry, and his company.

If he could ingratiate himself with Royce, it was good insurance. Royce was an ally who could save him and his company loads of money. He might even be able to help him with some less-than-legitimate personal enterprises in which he was involved. One hand washes the other, as they say.

"Yes, Sir. I don't think that will be a problem. Send me what you need and I'll get it done."

"Thanks, Mark. I knew I could count on you. Please let me know how I can help you with anything that comes up for American Pacific here in Washington."

Royce hung up, a smile of satisfaction on his lips. He was about to become a very wealthy man.

Mexican Jungle

A few weeks after the meeting between Senator Royce and Pablo Vazquez, a convoy of five semi-tractor trailer loads of pharmaceuticals arrived at a large, non-descript industrial complex after dark. The warehouse, which was the largest of the buildings, 5 kilometers off the main road and accessible only by a narrow, twisting road that was little more than a driveway in width, was hidden under camouflage netting and was patrolled by men carrying M-4 carbines, both in vehicles and on foot.

On the rooftop were two sandbagged positions. Inside each was a .50 caliber machine gun and several Stinger shoulder-launched anti-aircraft missile launchers. Any Mexican government helicopter venturing near would simply disappear in a flash.

El Carnicero called the drivers and warehouse men together. Altogether, the group totaled 19 men.

"I congratulate the drivers. You each have earned a nice bonus today!"

Cerveza flowed and the celebration went on for about 30 minutes. Half the drivers were intoxicated by now after supplementing the beers with whiskey or vodka. The atmosphere was like a fiesta as everyone drank, laughed and celebrated a successful haul of drugs.

"Now, however, we have some business to do. Jaime, come here," bellowed Vasquez.

El Carnicero motioned to one of the warehouse workers.

Nervously, 25-year-old Jaime Perez approached the man they called "Jefe," or boss.

"Ah, Jaime. I thought you were well-paid to work here in my warehouse, no?" Vasquez put his arm around the young man's shoulders and looked out at the group of men in front of him.

"Si, Jefe." The young man's eyes flashed with concern that quickly became fear.

"But I guess you thought you are not paid enough."

Vasquez nodded at two large men. Each man grabbed one of Jaime's arms. A third man brought a long, narrow table and ropes to the front of the room.

The men wrestled the wiry young man onto the table as he pleaded in vain for them to release him. In a moment, his back was down and his head dangled off one end of the gray metal table. His arms were quickly tied out at his sides and to yellow, vertical pipes cemented into the floor used to cordon off and stack pallets of drug shipments. Ropes around his torso soon secured him to the table.

Now, Jaime's face was flooded with panic. The men standing around watching wore similar looks. A large floor fan spun nearby, its clicking the only audible sound as Jaime, and everyone else, awaited El Carnicero's next words.

"Jaime, what is this?" Vasquez motioned to a box that two men carried in.

———٭———

"Jefe, jefe, I only…" Jaime sputtered, recognizing a large, green and white carton.

"It is a box of Oxycontin. It is the box you hid in the jungle. It is MY box, one that you stole from me. Did you think you would sell it?" Now, a visibly flushed Vasquez was yelling, the veins in his forehead protruding and his nostrils flaring.

"Jefe, por favor, por favor. It was for my wife and baby, and the new one due in two months."

"Ah yes, your poor wife and your children. It is a shame. But only an idiot tries to take what is mine!"

Vasquez gestured to a man to his left. The man pulled the starting rope on a gas chainsaw. He revved its motor twice loudly to be sure it would not stall, then handed it to El Carnicero.

Vasquez revved the motor again and waved the spinning chainsaw first in front of the gathered drivers and warehouse workers with theatrical flair, then closer to the young man writhing in vain on the table. He seemed to enjoy handling the powerful tool.

"Did you steal the box with this hand, la izquierda,?" Vasquez asked Jaime, motioning to the man's left hand.

"Well then…" and holding the saw, El Carnicero lopped off the poor boy's arm at the elbow. Grinding sounds filled the warehouse.

———٭———

Jaime screamed in agony. Two men vomited nearby as arterial blood flowed onto the floor in copious torrents.

"Or was it with la derecha?" again, Vasquez lowered the revving chainsaw, severing Jaime's right arm as the man wiggled and strained against the ropes and nearly passed out from the pain. Men murmured, cursed and some prayed aloud, "Dios Mio!"

"NOBODY steals from me!" yelled the aptly named El Carnicero as he revved the saw to its full speed and brought the spinning chain slowly and dramatically across Jaime's neck. The poor man's head bounced on the concrete floor and rolled toward one nearby man, who wretched and turned around so as not to see the horror before him. One man fainted and crumpled to the floor. Several cried openly.

"Now, does anyone else want to steal from me?" Vasquez asked in a low voice.

"No, Jefe!" shouted a chorus of dazed, half-drunken, frightened men, some staring at the pool of blood and others trying hard not to look.

"The crocodiles in the swamp will have a feast tonight," El Carnicero said.

GROWING THE BUSINESS

Pablo Vasquez was a cruel, cold, calculating man. But when it served his purposes, he could be a very patient man. It had taken him two years to develop a network of contacts in the U.S. at the leading pharmaceutical companies. These were fairly low-level contacts, all of whom had specific knowledge of the company shipping schedules and content.

Shipping and receiving supervisors earned a low- to-middle income wage. Getting paid thousands of dollars in under-the-table, tax-free income just for providing information about how many cartons of certain prescription medications would be shipping on a particular date, and to what destinations, was easy money. Usually, this information was available to Vasquez weeks or even months in advance.

Companies that led the market in the manufacture of drugs for erectile dysfunction were among the companies he had targeted, along with companies producing expensive cancer-fighting drugs; fertility drugs; antibiotics and numerous others. Companies that made the more expensive drugs were the ones that Vasquez had prioritized, as any good businessman would.

Armed with this knowledge, Vasquez and his associates were able to produce, package and deliver the counterfeit medications in time to switch them at the rail yards. In some cases, truck depots were the exchange locations. It was a comprehensive web of logistics.

On the production side, Vasquez's modern facilities included warehouses full of the necessary bottles and vials, labels and cartons—all exact or nearly exact replicas of the real thing in size, shape, color and labeling.

Not all senior Mexican police were corrupt and willing to take payoffs from Vasquez to avoid locating any of his production and shipping operations, but it wasn't at all difficult to find those who were. Vasquez, through a combination of bribes and threats of violence to police and their family members, had ensured that his operations would be unimpeded.

The one aspect of his counterfeiting operation that had eluded Vasquez up until now was the fact that he didn't have the capability to produce and package any liquid medication copies. He didn't have the necessary equipment or facilities. But he knew who did.

For months, he had been thinking about expanding his counterfeiting operations. What he had developed already was a talented work force, a collection of modern facilities and an extensive array of contacts, all made possible by the constant inflow of revenue from global sales of the drug products he seized.

But El Carnicero was an ambitious man. He knew that to his south, in the equally dense jungles of Guatemala, another successful counterfeiting enterprise also was flourishing.

Santino Trejo headed an enterprise that was miniscule compared to what Vasquez had created. However, Trejo had found a niche in the market for counterfeit liquid medications like cough syrups; drugs produced for those with difficulty swallowing; pediatric formulations and more. While he also produced some pills, mainly Viagra knockoffs, his operations in that part of his counterfeiting were far less successful than those of Vasquez. His was primarily a bottling operation.

Through the Latino criminal grapevine to which he and Trejo both kept tabs on each other and everyone else making a profit illegally, Vasquez made it known that he wanted to meet to discuss a possible merger. He would offer Trejo a significant cash incentive in return for a chance to buy some of Trejo's liquid counterfeits on a regular basis.

By becoming a major customer of Trejo's goods, Vasquez would be helping a competitor. In the short term, Vasquez planned to add these to the products he passed on to the U.S. military pharmacy system and other recipients, while the originals would join his other global shipments. He knew his overseas profits on the authentic medications would more than offset what he paid Trejo for the counterfeits.

At present, all liquid medications produced by the U.S. pharmaceutical companies and intercepted by Vasquez's organization were passed on to their intended recipients without any action by Vasquez. That represented lost potential revenue.

Of course, while he hoped Trejo would cooperate with this proposal, at least for a while, Vasquez planned to kill Trejo and his top assistants in time and to take over that entire criminal enterprise, making it part of his own, expanding empire.

In the meantime, he figured that being a regular source of income for Trejo would keep his competition from getting any similar ideas. Also, Trejo must certainly know El Carnicero's reputation for dealing with anyone who tried to cross him. Vasquez counted on that.

It wasn't long before word got back to Vasquez that Trejo was interested enough to discuss Vasquez' proposal. "How much are you willing to pay?" was of course the first question Trejo had.

Trejo provided Vasquez with a phone number so they could make initial contact with each other, and the deal was made. Vasquez now could flood the military pharmacy system and others with counterfeit medications in liquid form as well as in the many types of pills he already produced.

This arrangement continued for nearly 6 months according to the plan Vasquez had formulated. Once again, Vasquez could be a very patient man. Then, one day, Santino Trejo and two of his top assistants went missing. They never reappeared. Vasquez no longer had to make any payments to Trejo for liquid counterfeit medications.

41

Interagency Cooperation

Larry Hendrick had sent all of the information he had compiled up the chain to his boss at I.C.E. There were numerous documents and quite a few computer files. Some of those contained audio-taped conversations. His boss, Allen Carter, had set them aside for a few days, but now had time to look over the data Larry had accumulated. Nothing popped out at him right away as being of concern in regard to ground or rail transportation over the past few weeks, at least nothing that gave any hint of human trafficking.

A couple of the conversations were hard to make out...probably bad cell phone connections, he thought. There was one audio file of just over 4 minutes in length, so since he didn't feel like spending too much time on that kind of thing at the moment, he decided to listen to it because it was brief. He listened as Robbins greeted Senator Henry Royce.

Then he heard, "Listen, I have some manufacturing constituents who are trying to save some money on transportation of shipments. In particular, there are a few of your railroad complexes where they prefer to have their goods sent so they can consolidate follow-on transportation. This would be a change in some cases from where they are going now.

The thing is, these changes need to be made without any fanfare and rerouting needs to be done automatically, like forwarding mail. There is a need for some, uh, discretion in that the shipments need to be rerouted without the senders or some other parties being aware or involved in the changes.

Is there a way that I could provide you with a list of shipments, say, each month, and ensure that the shipments go only to the stations on the list, despite what the original shipping destination might be? Let's just call it selective rerouting."

Allen couldn't believe what he was hearing. First of all, he couldn't believe Mark Robbins, whom he'd known casually for years, would even entertain something like what the senator asked. Secondly, he was absolutely shocked that a U.S. senator was involved in something that sounded so shady. He needed to think about this and decide what to do next.

Allen Carter listened to the audio file several more times over the next two days. There was no mistaking it. Senator Royce had asked American Pacific Railroads executive Mark Robbins to do something illegal and Robbins had agreed to do it.

Before confronting Robbins, Carter decided to make a couple of phone calls. He was not aware that the D.E.A. also was monitoring American Pacific Railroad. Nonetheless, he knew that what he'd heard on the audio file would be something that one or more federal agencies would want to know about. He did not yet know about suspicions that Robbins also was involved in human trafficking.

Leaving work an hour early—telling his secretary he had a doctor's appointment—he drove to a nearby park, parked in a shady spot under some tall maple trees, and looked up the number for the D.E.A..

He got transferred twice, but when he identified himself as the head of American Pacific Railroad, the D.E.A. staffer decided he was important and put him through to the appropriate person.

Carter explained what he had in his possession and the D.E.A. official asked him to send him the files. Carter did so from home that evening and waited to hear back from D.E.A. Several days went by and he got a call at his office from an F.B.I. agent, telling him to say nothing to Robbins and to do nothing at all.

The agent said I.C.E. was working on the case in conjunction with the D.E.A. and the F.B.I. also was looking into it but not taking any action until everyone figured out what was going on. Those agencies did not want to arouse any suspicions. Carter agreed and left the matter in their hands.

The D.E.A., hearing of alleged involvement by a U.S. senator in something illegal that might involve counterfeit drugs, took an immediate interest in finding out more about what was going on. Because of the likelihood of federal crimes crossing state boundaries, the F.B .I. was contacted and now took the lead.

In time, Director Jim Barker was made aware of the ongoing investigation, due to the likelihood that the F.B.I. lab at Quantico, Virginia, would become involved in testing shipments to determine whether counterfeit pharmaceuticals were being sent to military installations. If so, the Naval Investigative Service, the U.S. Army Criminal Investigation Command and the other service counterparts also would become involved.

CHAPTER 42

Near Abu Kama, Iraq

A small, gasoline-powered generator whined and sputtered, its raucous sound and gray smoke partially masked by the low, crude mud and stone wall behind which it belched out its fumes. Inside the squalid meeting room in this tiny village, a distribution center for supplies going on to Raqqa, ISIS' capital of its new self-proclaimed caliphate, Aahil Farid sipped the locally favored mint tea, stroking the puffy red, oozing wound on his left cheek as he conversed with the other ISIS fighters. Two light bulbs hung from a wire, illuminating the room with sinewy shadows. Nearly 30 men had gathered to discuss recent battles, as well as to plan for new engagements against Kurdish and Iraqi forces.

Wounds, sometimes minor but often grievous, were not uncommon amongst these Jihadist warriors. Coalition airstrikes, drone strikes, artillery fire and small-arms skirmishes all had taken their toll on the 20,000 or so holy warriors streaming in from Libya, Pakistan, Morocco, Saudi Arabia and even Germany, France and the UK. A few were Americans.

Pouring a second cup of tea into his chipped brown pottery cup, Farid rummaged through a tattered leather bag hanging from his waist and extracted a bottle of pills. Shaking the bottle, he grinned and said, "Thank you, America!" His friend Mohammed laughed. Farid took out a Keflex pill and swallowed it with a sip of the fragrant tea. He would do this four times today, as the doctor had ordered.

ISIS' Jihadist fighters had their own doctors—volunteers from Egypt, Saudia Arabia and other Arab countries. Like the fighters, they believed that Islam should and would take over the world to become the one, universal religion, as they had been taught it should.

While ISIS hated the West and all that it represents, their zeal for establishing an Islamic world order did not blind them to the reality that U.S.-made pharmaceuticals were among the best in the world.

On the Black Market, ISIS was able to obtain powerful medications including antibiotics like Keflex, along with scores of others. Amply funded by ISIS' petroleum sales, its available pharmacy rivaled that of many developing countries. The irony that the enemy's medicines would keep Farid and others like him in the fight against "The Great Satan" and its proxies was not lost on him and his fellow fighters.

After traveling by truck and rail to the gulf port of Brownsville in Texas, Farid's antibiotics had joined tons of other pharmaceuticals aboard a cargo ship flying the flag of Panama. The ship transited the Atlantic and unloaded its hold at the container terminal in Tartus, Syria. From there, cargo, including Farid's Keflex, was trucked to one of numerous distribution centers controlled by ISIS.

Shooters

It was just beginning to rain, and it would be dark before long. Mike finished meeting with his client, who lived near Williamsburg, and decided to take the rural Route 5 back toward Richmond. It would be better than sitting in traffic on I-64, and he always enjoyed the beautiful, tree-lined country road as it wound its way through the dense, scenic woods to the east of Richmond.

A few other vehicles joined him at first, but after a while, he was alone, picking his way through the growing darkness. Ghost's headlights probed ahead, illuminating the many curves in the road. He used his high-beams as much as he could, knowing that at dusk, deer and other animals often could be seen in this area. Catching a glint in his rear-view mirror, Mike saw the headlights of another car behind him. Seconds later, the vehicle was much closer, obviously traveling very fast. There was no place for the car behind him to pass, so Mike sped up a bit, but so did the car behind him.

He tried speeding up and then slowing down. He tapped his brakes once or twice. The car behind him now was really tailgating him, and there weren't any passing zones on this road. Annoyed, all he could do was drive at a bit above the speed limit and hope the car would give him some more room. It was annoying, but not something he had not experienced before with other cars in the area. Tailgating was almost a daily occurrence.

———·——

Suddenly, Ghost's rear window burst, and Mike heard the unmistakable pop of gunfire that he'd heard many times before as a Marine. Then, Ghost swerved. Mike realized his left rear tire had been hit by a bullet. No mistaking it now, whoever was behind him was trying to cause him to crash—or worse.

With a flat tire, he knew he couldn't outrun the car. As he fought to keep control of Ghost on the road, his headlights showed a deer scrambling from right to left across the road about 20 yards ahead of him. Mike rounded a curve, and as he did so, he saw that the rest of a herd of deer, maybe seven or eight others, were crossing the road behind him, and in front of the oncoming car. Maybe it would slow them down just enough.

Mike sped up as much as the flat allowed, ran Ghost onto the right side of the road, turned off the headlights and grabbed the keys out of the ignition. He bolted across the road into the woods on the opposite side of the road, throwing himself prone into the vegetation and mud.

Mere seconds later, slowed by the deer herd, the shooters careened around the corner and onto the shoulder of the road behind Ghost, and as Mike had hoped, the two men, pistols in their hands, immediately jumped out and ran to look inside the Mercedes, then ran into the woods to the right of the car, convinced that Mike had run there to hide.

He could hear them yelling and calling to each other. He waited a minute, then found a rock the size of a lemon, and crouching low, hurled it far into the woods on the other side of the road, in front of the two men.

Immediately, gunfire followed as one of the men fired in the direction of the sound. Mike waited another minute, then threw another rock. This time, it sounded as though both men fired.

Mike slowed his breathing and tried to remain calm. Formulating a plan, he quickly smeared his face and hands with mud, grabbed a long, narrow branch, and crouching low, ran quickly to the shooters' car. He looked inside…no keys. Damn!

Removing his tie, Mike stuffed the wide end into the gas tank with the stick, pushing the cloth in as far as he could while still holding on to the narrow end of the tie. Pulling the tie out, he used the wide end, now soaked with gasoline, to paint the entire length of the tie quickly with the fuel.

Stuffing the wide end back in, he left about four inches of the narrow end sticking out of the gas tank, and taking the cigar lighter Special –in-Charge Barker had given him out of his pocket, lit it like a fuze.

Running as fast as he could, weaving and staying low, he worked his way as deeply as possible into the woods that had hidden him from the shooters.

Suddenly, smoke and a burst of flame shot out of the gas tank's opening. Then, with a rumbling explosion that reminded him of an 81 millimeter mortar shell bursting, the car mushroomed into a giant fireball, accompanied by a loud WHOOSH and a blast of heat that Mike felt, even through the vegetation, nearly 20 yards away.

"Now you're stuck out here, too," Mike thought. But then he realized the two shooters would guess by now that he was in the woods on the opposite side of the road, and would be coming for him.

It was getting darker. He decided the safest thing to do was to lie still and to camouflage himself and stay as quiet as possible. Without flashlights, it would be hard for the shooters to find him. Hopefully, they would give up their search and try to stop an oncoming car at some point to carjack it and get away. His dark gray suit and deep blue shirt would be fine camouflage.

Now that his tie was gone, and his top shirt button had come off when he removed the tie so quickly, his tee shirt provided a strip of white that he knew was like a neon sign. Mike packed mud on his neck and chest, covering the undershirt's top. He poked leaves and small twigs onto his back and shoulders and lay prone beside a small outcropping.

He again consciously slowed his breathing, taking deep, deliberate breaths and exhaling as infrequently as possible. He could hear the shooters, calling him, taunting him to come out. They thrashed through the woods around him. At one point, Mike felt the presence of one of the men within just a few yards of him in the dark, but he remained undetected.

After about 15 minutes, it seemed, the thrashing stopped. Mike thought the men had given up and returned to the road. Slowly, as quietly as he could, he crept to the road and darted back into the woods on the side where the men's car blazed, now some 75 yards behind him. He pushed deeper and deeper into the woods, sweeping the area in front of his face with one hand and feeling the ground in front of him with a long branch to avoid stepping off a slope, or even worse, a cliff.

He remembered a night tactical exercise at Quantico when he'd been poked in the eye by a branch he didn't see in the darkness, and that same night, another lieutenant had fallen, breaking an ankle in the process.

Mike hadn't heard the men for at least 10 minutes. He knelt low behind a large tree and for the first time, dared to reach for the cell phone in his pocket, hoping it was still there. His muddy hands curled around the phone, and shielding the screen's light inside his jacket, he dialed 911.

"Charles City County 911, what is your emergency?"

"I can't talk long." He whispered into the phone.

"I'm in the woods off Route 5, heading west, maybe a hundred yards from the car fire. Two men are shooting at me. Send help. Hurry, please." He hung up and turned the volume on the phone down to vibrate in case the dispatcher called him back. No need to broadcast his position now.

He stayed still for a few minutes, and hearing nothing, continued through the woods. A few minutes later, he could vaguely make out what looked like the form of a house or store. It was a cleared area off a small, dirt and gravel road that seemed to parallel Route 5.

He stopped in the wood line and watched the area for a few minutes, trying to make out any details through the darkness. There were no lights, meaning the structure was either closed or abandoned, most likely.

Exhausted now, his heart pouncing, he decided to make a dash toward the structure to see what it was. Maybe there would be the possibility of finding something he could use as a weapon. The place was abandoned and ramshackle. There was what was left of a small country store, with a storage shed behind it. He checked the shed, but found nothing of use as he groped around the inside in the dark, afraid to use his cell phone here for light.

A few minutes passed, and he heard a car coming. It stopped. Excited about the prospect of help, he watched to see who got out. His heart sank when he could finally make out the fact that instead of police or the sheriff, four men with guns had emerged, one of them yelling, "Find him!"

Mike couldn't be sure, but it looked as though some of them were armed with rifles. He crept slowly into the woods behind the shed and hid, lying prone.

Powerful flashlights pierced the darkness all around him. Light danced off the ground and off the trees, making the night seem even more ominous. He lay motionless.

Minutes passed, and it seemed that the thumping of his heart rivaled the sounds of men crashing through the dense foliage. Maybe they would give up looking for him. More minutes passed and he began to think he might be okay here until morning light, at which point the men would surely find him.

Suddenly, a beam of light passed over him.

"I think he's over here!" one man yelled.

Several men ran toward the shed. He was caught.

Rescued

The man shouting orders picked him up roughly by his jacket and the four men walked him toward the road, cursing. Now Mike saw the pistol pointed at him.

"Nice try, and that was a neat trick, blowing up our car, asshole, but it didn't get you anywhere," one of the original shooters said mockingly. He was a bald, swarthy man with several days of growth on his face. His accent sounded Northeastern...New Jersey, maybe.

"This is it," Mike thought. He was scared, but somehow resolved to what was coming.

"Jesus save me," he prayed silently.

"You and your girlfriend really should have kept your noses out of other peoples' business, you piece of shit," said the leader.

"You asked too many questions and got too many people nervous."

"If you hurt Kimberly, there won't be any place on this planet where her father won't find you," Mike said.

"Yeah, I'm really worried about that," said the

emed to be in charge.

nce, in the distance, the sound of si-
oser and closer. Mike saw red and blue
hts coming down the road from both
The unmistakable WHUMP WHUMP
WHUMP of a helicopter grew deafeningly loud.

Suddenly, a wide, brilliant spotlight shined down as the helicopter hovered directly above.

"F.B .I.-- throw down your weapons and don't move!" came the order over the chopper's loud-speaker.

One of the men fired at the helicopter. A red laser beam from the aircraft found his chest, simultaneously with a three-round burst from a special agent's M-4 carbine. The man fell dead. Another of the four turned to run, but a burly Prince George County Sheriff's deputy met him with a Remington 12 gauge pump shotgun pointed at his chest. He decided to stop.

The bald man dropped his weapon, an Israeli Uzi, and raised his hands.

The fourth man, the leader, was closest to Mike and grabbed him by the arm.

Pointing a pistol at Mike, he began to back away, using Mike's body as a shield as he took him hostage, hoping to escape.

Mike's Marine Corps martial arts training kicked in before he could even think about what to do. As the man took a step back, making himself momentarily off balance, Mike reached with his left hand for the wrist of the gun hand, immobilizing it as he raised the arm, and the gun, toward the sky. Quickly turning his right hip into the man, and reaching back and grabbing his jacket with his right hand, Mike pulled him forward, throwing him to the ground as the pistol flew harmlessly onto the ground, landing in the mud with a thud.

Another laser illuminated the would-be shooter's chest as he lay on the ground, a small, red dot making irregular circles on his shirt. Upon seeing it, he threw his arms to the side and stayed motionless until a deputy rolled him onto his face in the muck and handcuffed his arms behind him.

The helicopter landed on the road as local law-enforcement officers handcuffed and placed the three surviving gunmen into patrol cars. F.B.I. agents wearing black tactical vests and body armor jumped out of the helicopter. One of them was Jim Barker.

"Nice work with that one!" Special Agent Sam Ridenour shouted to Mike as the helicopter's rotors gradually slowed.

"Semper Fi! That was a nice move!," Barker said, shaking Mike's muddy hand.

"How the hell did you get here so fast?" Mike asked, unashamedly throwing his arms around Barker, forgetting that he was filthy and wet.

"Well, it seems as though these guys installed a GPS transmitter in your car. When we figured out what was going on, and who these guys were that were so interested in you and Kimberly, so did we. But I also had already had one installed in that cigar lighter I gave you," he said with a grin.

"Wow! I liked it before, but it's REALLY my favorite thing, now!" Mike laughed.

"We've been monitoring your location for weeks on a daily basis. Your suspicions were right all along. Our lab verified that the two medications your friend was taking were counterfeit. One had miniscule traces of the real drug in it, along with a bunch of crap that didn't belong in it. The other one was nothing but a placebo. We knew for sure then that this had to be a big counterfeiting ring with some kind of major connections to get counterfeit drugs into the military pharmacy system. We were staying very close to you and Kimberly after the trouble you both ran into with your apartments.

When your GPS signal stopped moving out here in the middle of nowhere, we figured something was up. Your 911 call helped, too. It confirmed your location for us. By the way," Barker said, "You look like hell."

Mike laughed, realizing that, caked with mud and with twigs sticking out of his suit, he must look like a swamp monster."Hey, the Marines taught us how to camouflage ourselves, right?

"Yeah, they sure did. I know they also taught us how to blow shit up!" We flew over quite a nice little fire."

"Oh, that. Yeah, that was the most fun I had tonight!"

"Let's get you cleaned up." Mike boarded the helicopter—the first one he'd been in since he left the Corps, and donned the hearing protectors an agent handed him. They lifted off. As they flew over the still blazing car and saw the flashing lights of a patrol car hauling one of the shooters off to jail, Mike was finally able to reflect on the past couple of hours.

Just then, Barker's cell phone rang and he strained to listen to the caller over the helicopter's rotor noise.

"Okay, great, thanks," he said.

Now that he was able to think, rather than concentrate on his own survival, Mike thought about the fact that these men had tried to kill him because of what he knew.

"I hope Kimberly's okay!" Mike said. "Maybe these guys were after her tonight, too."

"They were," Barker replied. But we've
followed for weeks. She's fine. Agents in
have two guys in custody there, and the two
car you turned into a barbecue pit also are
tody. Well, the one who decided to surrende . ine
other one is D.O.A. That's what that phone call was
about."

The helicopter landed at Fort Eustis, a nearby
Army base. A soldier showed Mike to a men's locker
room and shower, and handed him soap and a towel.
Later, the Army gave him an olive drab jump suit
to put on, and his shoes, which had been cleaned of
the mud that he'd collected in the woods. He had no
underwear other than the muddy ones he'd worn,
so under the clean jump suit he was "commando,"
as the saying goes.

His wallet, watch and the cigar lighter were returned to him. All had been cleaned up a bit, but the
wallet still had some caked mud inside.

Mike sat in a lounge. Another soldier offered the
F.B.I. agents and Mike coffee.

"Here," Barker said.

He handed Mike a cigar and opened the wrapper on one for himself.

"Allow me," Mike said, lighting the agent's cigar
and then his own.

"God, how I love this lighter!"

Barker laughed. "Now, that's living," he said,
exhaling the bluish-white cloud.

"Amen. I wasn't sure I'd ever smoke another cigar again. That would have been a shame!"

"Uh-huh. Only a cigar smoker would understand
that, but I do," Barker said, blowing a smoke ring
that expanded and then disappeared into a wispy
haze.

Mike rested for about a half hour. Barker left
the room to make a few calls. When he returned, he
had news.

Taking Down the Counterfeiters

"Senator Royce from California, some trucking company executives, a railroad company bigwig and some Big Pharma guys--and some others, about 20 altogether, have been arrested across the country. Mexican authorities have arrested another bunch down there, including the head of the cartel that was doing the counterfeit drug switching...a guy named Vasquez.

Apparently, there was a real gun battle down there when the Mexican police closed in on the counterfeiters. They had some heavy weapons. The police took some casualties but killed a lot of the drug guys. They think they might have either killed or captured them all," Barker said.

"Amazing. Whoever would have thought that one of my clients dying would lead to all this?" Mike shook his head in disbelief.

"It wouldn't have without you and Kimberly, plain and simple. Based on your suspicions, you two really broke this case. We just followed your lead. Especially after Kimberly discovered that one counterfeit medication at Great Lakes, we knew somehow, someone was getting fake drugs into the military pharmacy system. We had a lucky break with I.C.E. sharing some information with us about a railroad exec involved in human trafficking and that kind of thing, and it went from there. When we got Senator Royce on audio about American Pacific Railroad, it all came together."

"I just never would have expected counterfeit medications to be such big business," Mike said.

"The lack of effective regulation of pharmaceuticals worldwide is really poor. The World Health Organization estimates that almost half of the global drug market is impacted by counterfeit medicines. Most of these fakes are found in what we'd call Third World countries…, especially throughout Asia and Africa." Barker explained.

Mike was amazed that the problem was so chronic.

"That's scary."

Barker shrugged. "It is, and lately, the problem is getting worse in Central America. With Mexico right on our southern border, and with the way the border is so porous, the D.E.A. is seeing more and more infiltration of fake drugs coming in from there. Everybody gets emotionally hung up on immigration, families being separated from kids and all that…but that's not the only problem down there.

Counterfeit drug operations are expanding in Asia, Africa and other parts of the globe, with billions of dollars, if not more, being made by drug lords who are turning more and more from the production and sale of narcotics to the production and sale of placebo or low-quality pharmaceuticals,"

Barker added.

"Internationally, law-enforcement agencies have traditionally focused their time, and prosecutors their efforts, on narcotics trafficking, so it's become less risky for the makers of counterfeit medications to ply their trade."

Mike couldn't wait to call Kimberly. Back at home courtesy of the F.B.I., he called her.

"Are you okay? They told me you're okay," he asked.

"Yeah, the F.B.I. was like the cavalry. They got to me just in time. What about you? Did the crooks come after you?" she asked.

"Oh, yeah! We did play hide and seek in the woods for about an hour. I made a nice little fire for them. I'll have to tell you all about it later. Your dad's friend, Jim Barker, and local cops got to me just in time, too. You won't believe this, but Jim had a tracking device in that cigar lighter he gave me!"

"I love technology!" Kimberly was yelling with excitement.

"Me, too."

His first call the following morning was to Cathy Kincaid.

"Cathy, it's Mike. I've got a lot to tell you! Can you put on a pot of coffee?"

"Yes, absolutely. Come on over."

She was excited and hoped Mike could give her information about why Marvin had died so suddenly. She also hoped someone, somehow, would be held accountable. She would not be disappointed.

A Career Ends

Sitting at the Sheffield's kitchen table in Chicago two weeks later, Mike tried to answer Kimberly's parents' questions as best he could.

"How did the F.B.I. figure out that Senator Royce was involved?" the general asked.

"That was great," Mike said. "It's really ironic, in a way. Royce was one of the people in Congress during the last administration who pushed for the National Security Agency to spy on everyone's telephone calls over the past few years. I guess he didn't know they'd be spying on members of Congress, too.

Not only that, but apparently some other agencies have been doing their own monitoring of people in top positions—like him. Jim Barker says lots of federal agencies are doing it—I.CE., the I.R.S., Homeland Security and others.

Because of the sensitive nature of some of the committees he serves on, he was being routinely monitored to be sure he wasn't divulging classified information, either intentionally or through carelessness. I guess they learned some things after that famous private email server debacle.

Then, on top of that, a conversation he had with the railroad executive who helped reroute the real prescription drugs was recorded as well, by I.C.E. That conversation was about counterfeit medications going to military installations, the military mail-order pharmacy and other locations,

---

The F.B.I. told me they didn't get much from his office or home phone lines, but they have recordings of him arranging for drug shipments to be directed to warehouses where counterfeit drugs from Mexico were substituted and shipped to the military hospitals and clinics for distribution.

Somehow, they were able to tap into cell phone calls he had with the head of the drug operation in Mexico. They have technology we can't even imagine. Barker said they can basically shoot an invisible laser beam at a window and record all the conversations taking place in that room based on the vibrations of the glass. It's wild.

Not only that, but Royce's administrative assistant was interviewed and provided significant incriminating information. She didn't start out being very cooperative, but Barker says that changed when she was threatened with charges and prison unless she cooperated fully with the federal investigation. She apparently had seen some documents and overheard some conversations that, when pressed, she had shared.

He also says that once the F.B.I. figured out what was going on with him, they also made arrangements to go through his trash at home. They found some discarded emails there that also incriminated him."

"That sounds like the evidence they'll need to convict him," Mrs. Sheffield said.

"For sure. Also, he apparently is actually the one who ordered the hits on Kimberly and me, so he'll go away for life for conspiracy to commit murder. At his age, he'll die in a federal penitentiary.

He found out about Kimberly's F.O.I.A. requests and knew we were digging for information that might eventually expose him. That's why he was so interested in our computers."

"So, what was in it for him?" the general asked.

"Money, and lots of it. The way Barker explained it to me, because the military pays the pharmaceutical companies a discounted price for drugs, a million dollars worth of prescriptions intended for TRICARE distribution points is worth maybe twice that, and four or five times that much on the illegal market.

The counterfeiters substituted cheap counterfeits worth a fraction of the millions of dollars of actual value, then sold the real drugs at marked up prices to overseas countries, some of which the U.S. doesn't do any business with. There are sheiks and ayatollahs and other dictators willing and able to pay whatever it costs to get the high-quality U.S. medications they want for themselves, their friends and family members, and anyone who supports their regime."

"So, the drug lords would make millions, and so would the senator and the various people in on the deal at the pharmaceutical manufacturers and railroad and trucking companies?" Mrs. Sheffield asked.

"Exactly, and guys like Senator Royce and the others in the administration, who have no regard for the military anyway, saw it as a way to pay themselves while also 'saving' millions of dollars in health care that would have been paid to veterans and their families.

Guys like Royce have no conscience. They were more than willing to sacrifice military veterans and even their spouses and kids. That way, they could then divert that money to pet projects in their state or district, helping them to keep getting re-elected and to collect 'donations' from corporations and wealthy individuals. In their minds, everybody wins."

"Everybody except the veterans and their families," Kimberly said.

"Why couldn't the bad guys just sell the counterfeit prescriptions overseas?" Mrs. Sheffield asked.

"Barker says it's because the people buying the drugs over there are very wealthy, very powerful, and very bad to have upset with you. Even the drug lords wouldn't be safe if they ripped off some of these folks," Mike answered.

"He also told me that all the information gathered during this investigation has been provided to the U.S. military and other government agencies. Knowing that the real drugs that counterfeits were substituted for are being shipped overseas to people who shouldn't be getting them is going to help target some of those folks, too. As a bonus, Barker told me the F.B.I. got information that helped them to stop some human trafficking activity in a couple of the border states. He was really happy about that, too."

47

Delray Beach, Florida

Mike spent Christmas with his mother and aunt in Florida and told them the whole story of the past year and how Kimberly and he had worked together to help discover and break up a major drug counterfeiting operation. But even he didn't realize that some of the purloined pharmaceuticals intended for military personnel and their families were still on their way to overseas destinations. That would be the case until the last stolen shipments were delivered. Most were on cargo ships, which would take weeks or longer to reach their destinations. Now that Senator Royce, his railroad contact and all of the others arrested were in custody, there would be an abrupt end to that supply chain.

While in Florida, Mike saw that Christmas sales were going on and there were some good deals on diamond engagement rings. It was something that had been on his mind for a while. He had hesitated to think about asking Kimberly to marry him for one main reason. She loved her new job in Chicago and was just getting settled there.

Not only that, but she had family there. He didn't think he could expect her to move to the Richmond area and give all that up. He looked at some rings, but didn't buy one. He could always do that in Richmond if he decided to, he thought.

For his part, he had no-one in Richmond. That's why when he got back home, he had decided to talk with Steve Miller, his boss at Archer Global Insurance Company. Steve made a few calls. There was an opening coming up at Archer's Chicago office. It would mean cultivating a whole new list of contacts in that area, but he still had a network of clients he could keep regardless of where he was based.

Back in Richmond again, he continued to think about all the pros and cons of moving to Chicago. The biggest pro was obvious...Kimberly.

He had a great idea and couldn't wait to see if Kimberly could break free for a few days.

Washington, D.C.

Kimberly had been able to convince her supervisor to let her have a long weekend. The quick flights to and from Richmond made even a day or two off from work seem like a mini-vacation.

Mike met Kimberly's flight at Reagan International Airport. Standing at the security check point near the Arrivals gate, he watched the passengers walk down the ramp and exit into the terminal building. Mothers with young children, elderly passengers with canes, a red-faced, large man with arms full of luggage and paper bags…and then he saw Kimberly, smiling, rushing to meet him.

Clear of the plane's exodus, they hugged and kissed. "We're both alive!" Kimberly said, rejoicing again that they'd both come out of the ordeal scared but unscathed.

"Thank God. I'm sorry I got you into that mess," Mike said.

"No! Don't you say that. We're a team. We needed to work together to do this. Think of all the people we've helped!"

After waiting for Kimberly's one checked suit-case, they walked to the parking garage.

"You got Ghost back!" Kimberly said.

"Of course! I can't let her go! I had the rear window replaced, got a new tire and had some body work done to patch a couple of bullet holes in the trunk, but now she's good as new. Well, good as she's been before getting shot up, anyway! She's a combat veteran now. I should have a Combat Action Ribbon painted on her!"

"That would be so cool. She's a survivor."

"So are we," Mike said, easing the Mercedes out of the garage, past the booth where he inserted the parking pass and his credit card, and into traffic. He headed for the hotel in Crystal City where he had a room reserved for the duration of the insurance conference he was attending. He had asked if she could make the trip, and she was able to get a few days off from work.

"My conference goes for three days," Mike told her. "I have to attend some of the sessions, but some are optional. I need to learn some of this stuff, but we can spend the evenings together, have dinner… and who knows what else?"

Her grin promised a lot.

"Sounds good to me," Kimberly said, squeezing Mike's shoulder.

Mike changed lanes and took the exit for the hotel. "Seems like it was just Thanksgiving. Can't believe New Years Eve has already come and gone!"

"I know. I was sorry we couldn't spend it together. I wish I had more time to spend with you."

"Yeah, me too, but Chicago isn't really all that far, especially by plane."

Mike drove out of the airport and headed toward Crystal City.

"There's something I want to show you," Mike said.

He made a small diversion to nearby Arlington, just a few blocks from the hotel. Pulling up in front of the U.S. Marine Corps Iwo Jima Memorial, honoring the historic World War II flag raising, he parked the car.

"Come with me," he said.

They both stood silently in front of the inspirational monument for a moment.

"You know, this monument reminds me of the smaller one outside the front gate at Quantico."

"Sure. They're exactly the same except that this one is so much bigger," Kimberly said. "It's so inspirational!"

"Yes, it is. I thought that since we met at Quantico and had so many great times there, this would be the perfect place."

At that, he slowly got down on one knee, took a ring case out of his pocket, and said, "Kimberly Sheffield, from the moment we first met, you have been my strength, my supporter, my partner and my best friend. And, we've grown to be much more together. We've been through more adventures already than most people have in a lifetime. I love you, I can never stop thinking about you, and I want to spend the rest of my life with you. And, before you answer, if you say yes, I have a job lined up with my company in Chicago. So, Kimberly, will you marry me?"

"Are you kidding me?! What do you mean IF I say yes? I never expected a proposal from you on this trip, but yes, yes, yes, yes!"

They hugged and kissed as a nearby crowd of visitors erupted in applause. It was a moment that they both couldn't wait to share with their families.

Somewhere in Nevada

Just as she did six days each week, Amanda Johnson awoke at 5 a.m. to the sound of loud rock music on her radio. Turning off the alarm, she stretched and waited for the second alarm clock to split the morning calm yet again five minutes later, this time with a shrill beeping sound.

While she hated getting up so early, she loved her job and didn't mind the 30-minute morning drive, which gave her time to clear her head and enjoy a cup of coffee and a cereal bar on the way.

Slim and tall, she had played basketball in high school and at the Georgia Institute of Technology, where she graduated with a degree in Aeronautical Engineering. She excelled in academics and graduated number 1 in her class.

After working as an intern at Pratt & Whitney for a year and a half, she returned to GIT and earned her Master's degree in Computer Science. There was a recruiting event on campus shortly after her graduate class completed the various Master's programs at GIT, and Amanda talked with several representatives of tech companies, as well as with a couple of government agencies. She even briefly chatted with U.S. Air Force recruiters, but didn't have a serious interest in joining the military.

As she was breaking off conversation with the Air Force recruiter, an Air Force colonel stopped by to check in with the recruiter. He greeted Amanda as well.

"Hello, I'm Colonel Hill, with the Air Force Recruiting Command. Are you ready to join the Air Force today?"

Amanda laughed nervously.

"Hello, I'm Amanda Johnson. No, I was just talking with Tech Sergeant Myers about aeronautics. I have a Master's in Computer Science and a B.S. in Aeronautical Engineering, but I'm not really interested in being in the military."

"That's too bad. That's the kind of background we're looking for, for sure."

"I know, but there are a lot of reasons why it wouldn't work for me. But, I have a couple of uncles who served in the military and I'm definitely patriotic. It's just not my thing, though."

"Well, the military lifestyle isn't for everyone. But with your credentials, there are other ways you could serve your country—even work at the Pentagon or one of many other installations—but as a civilian."

Colonel Hill was an impressive officer. An African-American about 40 years old, he was solidly built and wore his uniform well as a representative of the Air Force. He was intelligent, well-spoken and friendly.

Amanda liked him and her curiosity was piqued by what he said.

"So, if I wanted to find out more about that kind of thing—working for the government as a civilian—what would I do to get more information?"

"For someone like you, with your background in both aeronautical engineering and computers, I'd start with NASA. But also, there's a bunch of others.

Check out some websites for starters. But here's my card. If I can help at all, let me know. I'd still like to get you in the Air Force, but I'll bet some agency will want to snap you up."

Amanda smiled, took the card and thanked him. Shaking hands with the colonel and Tech Sergeant Myers, she made her way past the recruiters, eager graduates and some parents there to support their newly minted grads.

As she drove away from the campus, she tossed the materials she'd gathered from a few of the organizations at the event on the passenger seat of her car and headed into traffic on Interstate 75.

The next week had been routine at Pratt & Whitney and while she wasn't earning much, it was a paid internship and she was learning a lot and meeting interesting people.

The phone call early one evening was a surprise.

"Amanda, hello. This is Colonel Randall Hill. I met you at the Tech event."

"Oh, yes, sir. Of course I remember you. How did you get my number?"

"You filled out a form at the recruiting event, remember?"

"Ah, that's right. What can I do for you? You and Sergeant Myers were great to talk to, but nope, I'm still not ready to enlist!"

"I know, and I'm disappointed. But, you really impressed me. Between your bachelor's and master's degrees and your internship experience, you really have some in-demand skills."

"Well, thank you."

"Listen, there's someone I think you might like to meet. He's pretty senior in his agency and I was talking with him the other day. I mentioned that I met you and thought you had a lot of potential for work in his organization. He's interested in talking with you."

"Oh. Well, that's really nice of you and I appreciate that you remembered me enough to think about me!"

"I meet lots of promising young people. Some stand out."

"Okay, now I'm blushing, I'm sure. How can I contact him?"

"He'll be contacting you. His name is Gary Fletcher."

"Thank you so much. What organization is he with?"

"He'll tell you. Good luck."

"Thanks again."

Amanda was surprised and curious about this "Gary Fletcher."

Four days passed and Amanda's cell phone rang while she was making dinner.

"Amanda, this is Gary Fletcher. Randy Hill mentioned me to you, I hope."

"Oh, yes, Sir, he did."

"He told me enough about you to spark my interest in you as someone my agency might be interested in. Can we possibly meet for lunch sometime this week?"

"Um, sure. I think I can get an extended lunch break one day. Where are you located?"

"Actually, I'm in Arlington, Virginia. But I want to meet you and I can be down in your area on either Thursday or Friday."

Amanda wasn't sure what to think. Why would Mr. Fletcher want to travel that far to meet her?

"May I ask what agency you're with?"

"Let's meet, okay? I'll tell you more then. You can call me at this number when you know which day works for you and I can meet you wherever you like. Let's make it someplace quiet, though, so we have a chance to talk. It can be a public place. Of course, since you don't know me, it can just be a quiet booth in the back of a restaurant, or even a couple of sandwiches on a bench in a park. I don't care about the food. I just want to meet you and see if you might be interested in some training we offer—paid of course."

"Okay, sure thing. Let me get back to you tomorrow about which day and I'll try to think of a good place to meet."

"Great. I look forward to hearing from you."

And so they had met and talked. It was a conversation that had momentous ramifications.

Fletcher had done his homework prior to their meeting. He knew, it seemed, EVERYTHING about Amanda, her family, her time with Pratt & Whitney, her years at Georgia Tech...even her basketball games and college boyfriends. He told her that, and so when he finally told her he was with the Central Intelligence Agency, she wasn't surprised how he knew it.

He shared with her that he and Colonel Hill were old friends and that he had a great deal of respect for him and his judgment. So, when Hill called him to say that he might have met the kind of person the CIA wanted to bring on board for a highly specialized type of work, Fletcher was eager to meet Ms. Amanda Johnson. That was even more true when Fletcher checked on her background, education and time with Pratt & Whitney, where she had wowed everyone she worked with due to her intelligence and judgment.

He had run checks on her financial status, her credit score, her driving record—all of it. And, he liked what he had found out about her. She was exactly what she seemed to be, a smart, dependable, trustworthy young American with an outstanding technical background in computer science and aeronautical engineering, along with strong Christian values. That last trait, perhaps, was the only thing that gave him pause.

He wondered. Would those Christian values keep Amanda from being willing or able to do the kind of work he was going to offer her?

C H A P T E R 5 0

Flying

letcher had given her an overview…just a glimpse, really…of what working for the C.I.A. in the capacity he had in mind would be like. She was shocked at first to think that somehow, this all had come to pass since that day on campus when she met the impressive Air Force officer who chatted with her about aeronautical engineering and computers in an effort to entice her to join the U.S. Air Force.

Make no mistake, Gary Fletcher was not someone who made this type of offer on behalf of the C.I.A. lightly, nor without high expectations. He had made it vividly clear to Amanda that if she embarked on the training program he was offering, there would be long months of studying, long days in simulators, long nights and sometimes unusual hours working, sometimes alone but usually with small teams of others.

The work would be difficult, vital—and highly classified way beyond Top Secret, Sensitive Compartmented Information. There was always the possibility that she would fail. But he didn't think that was going to happen, and neither did Amanda. They both were right.

Now, three years later, when she reflected on that lunch meeting with Gary Fletcher, Amanda realized what a blur the intervening time had been, and just how much that meeting had changed her life, and the lives of so many others.

The long months of training were far behind her now. She was a full-fledged C.I.A. operator. She had made the move to a small suburb of Las Vegas. Her neighbors thought she worked in Information Technology. She did, but they had no idea how and where, nor could they ever find out.

In the dimly lit, futuristic-looking facility she reported to each day, Amanda was the only woman on a team of eight people. She also was the youngest of the group, but had earned the respect and confidence of the others during the two years she had been working with them.

Amanda controlled a $17 million General Atomics MQ-9 Reaper drone. Using a satellite link with only a few seconds of delay, she flew the unmanned aircraft that carried a variety of weapons including laser-guided bombs, Hellfire II air-to-ground missiles, missiles effective against enemy aircraft, and cameras capable of providing the operator with unprecedented clarity from high above, where the Reaper flew at altitudes undetectable from the ground.

Before she could fly the Reaper, Amanda first had to obtain a private pilot's license, then complete months of simulator training with the MQ-9 Reaper UAV Ground Control System. All this had been the most challenging academic course of study she had ever completed.

51

Destinies Converge

The drive to work had been uneventful, with light traffic in the early morning hours. By 7 a.m., Amanda was well-settled into her work station, her pink ceramic mug of coffee sending small swirls of steam into the air. She wrapped her hand around the mug, its warmth and bumpy texture soothing her like a brief but welcome spa treatment. The only sound was the slight hum of computers.

In the busy seaport of Tartus, Syria, 7,180 miles away, it was 5 p.m. and the cacophony of cranes lifting huge containers from the cavernous holds of merchant ships, truck horns blaring and port laborers yelling in Arabic, showed no signs of the workday ending.

Omar Ahmad, 24, drummed the steering wheel with his fingers, waiting impatiently in a line of 11 trucks as the black and tan, Panamanian-flagged ship unloaded its contents onto the dock with its massive crane. Smaller cranes, some stationary and some mounted on large trucks, moved the containers into staging areas or directly onto waiting vehicles in a constant stream of activity and noise.

7:12 a.m., Las Vegas, U.S.A.

Amanda scanned the screens that illuminated her work station with a dim glow of red, green and white lights. The various screens provided data about weather conditions around the globe, as well as satellite and aircraft images of terrain, wind velocity at different altitudes, radar sweeps and much more.

After consulting some charts and inputting data using her keyboard, she began to concentrate the multiple images into coverage of a small sector of Syria, specifically the large port city of Tartus.

5:12 p.m. Tartus, Syria

Omar's old, white Toyota truck trembled slightly as it idled. It was almost as though it sensed his nervousness and reacted accordingly. He had picked up cargo in Tartus, as well as at the main port in Leticia, to the north, half a dozen times, but he always felt somewhat nervous doing it. The first time, he had an older Egyptian man as a mentor, but after that, he had been a solo operator. Such was the case today as he waited to pick up a truckload of cargo bound for Ar Raqqah, 390 kilometers to the North East.

The drive would take him nearly 6 hours, meaning that most of it would be in the dark. It would be several more hours in Tartus, he thought, before he would be loaded up and able to leave the port.

7:37 a.m., Las Vegas, U.S.A

One of Amanda's team members, Craig, handed her a briefing folder. Like almost everything she handled at work, it was marked **CLASSIFIED— TOP SECRET, SCI**, meaning Sensitive Compartmented Information. In it was information gathered from a host of intelligence sources, both human and electronic. A member of another, partnering team had summarized the findings in several paragraphs that Amanda read slowly several times, carefully digesting the material.

Over the past several days, her team had been concentrating on surveillance of the coastal areas of Syria. Intelligence sources had identified that weapons, equipment and other supplies had been arriving at Syria's port cities and then been transferred by ground transportation to ISIS fighters elsewhere in the country. The workers at the port had no idea that the Reaper's technology allowed Amanda and other pilots to see details so fine that they could distinguish one individual from another at altitudes that made the drone invisible to those on the ground.

6:57 p.m., Tartus, Syria

Omar was now number 8 in line. He hoped that the next few vehicles would load quickly, as the last 3 had. The waiting was always the worst part. When he was driving, he felt more confident than when he was sitting still in the port. His instructions were to pick up crates of detonators, GPS devices and medications and deliver them to his contact in Ar Raqqah, the ISIS-proclaimed capital of the caliphate they were forming with each new conquest in the region.

Omar had no way of knowing that some of the pharmaceuticals he would be picking up had come all the way from one of the ports in Texas, to which an unscrupulous American Pacific Railroads executive had diverted them at the request of a greedy, long-tenured American senator and a ruthless Mexican drug kingpin.

7:52 p.m., Tuesday, Tartus, Syria

Omar was now number 3 in line. The first truck ahead of him was a large one and he expected that it would take a while for it to be loaded. The one directly in front of him was a pickup truck, like his, and should not take too long.

He was getting less nervous now and settling in, mentally preparing himself for the drive he would be doing soon.

His truck smelled like cinnamon from the gum he was chewing. Sitar music played on the radio. Arabic newspapers were scattered on the seat next to him and on the floor of the passenger side. He had kept busy reading those but now just waited, peering ahead through the windshield in expectation.

Thirty five minutes passed and then a middle aged, bearded man with a clipboard approached his truck. Omar produced some documents he'd been given and handed them to the man, who studied them carefully and then walked away without speaking.

9:52 a.m., Tuesday, Nevada, USA

Amanda ran some remote systems checks on her bird—a term she and her co-workers often used to describe the drones they piloted. All systems were working perfectly and the drone was in the air not far from Tel Aviv, Israel. She had lifted off from a secret Israeli Air Force base about an hour ago and was high above the Mediterranean Sea, following the coastline as the drone headed North.

8:40 p.m., Tuesday, Tartus, Syria

Finally! Omar exhaled a long puff of smoke from his British Lambert & Butler cigarette. The truck in front of him was moving out of line, its bed full of crates. It was Omar's turn to accept the supplies he'd come for. Another bearded man in a long, white robe commonly worn in this Arab nation yelled to Omar to move up, directing him to park underneath a large, orange crane.

10:40 a.m., Tuesday, Nevada, USA

Amanda sipped her Diet Coke and munched on a package of pretzels from one of the vending machines down the hall. The agency kept them stocked, because the 24-hour-a-day operations gave the operators the munchies at all hours of the day and night. There were chips, cookies, popcorn, pretzels...something for every taste.

Amanda's Reaper was high above the coast of Syria now, far above any detection or shoot-down ability the Syrian's had, even with their Russian-supplied anti-aircraft systems. The drone also had numerous classified, high-tech attributes—radar reflecting paint and others—that made it virtually impossible to spot when it was that high.

Omar inched the Toyota up to where he was told to wait for a crane to position pallets in his truck, assisted by two young men who guided the slowly swinging cargo into place. A few soft banging and scraping sounds told him they were getting the items into the truck bed.

One of the young men yelled loudly to the crane operator and he retracted the long cable that had been released by the other young man, who had climbed atop the cargo to unhook it.

9:17 p.m., Tuesday, Tartus, Syria

Omar waited in line again as a few trucks ahead of him made their way out from the gated port onto the local roads. Once clear of the compound, he followed signs for Highway M1, which would take him to Homs, and then to Route 42 and east to his destination.

11:17 a.m. Nevada, USA

Amanda had been watching the activity at the port of Tartus for the past two hours, ever since her drone had arrived over the coastline. A few ships had come and gone from Tartus. She could clearly see the ships' names and the flags they flew. She had checked her intel sheets, but none were subjects of any interest to the C.I.A.

1:42 a.m., Wednesday, Syria, somewhere along

Route 42

Omar was still driving on in the dark now after several hours, heading for the intersection with Route 6 North, which would take Omar and the three other trucks that were all headed for Resafa, Alhora and ultimately, Ar Raqqah. From Tartus to the Resafa intersection, at night on this road, would take about six hours. He would sleep there tonight, then drive on into Iraq in the morning to his final delivery destination, Al-Mawsil, where one of ISIS' distribution centers was located.

Omar rubbed his eyes, popped another piece of cinnamon gum in his mouth and drove on through the dark. Every once in a while, he caught a glimpse of one of the trucks ahead of him, and only once, in his rearview mirror, of the one behind him. He would soon reach the Resafa intersection.

3:42 p.m., Tuesday, Nevada, USA

In the dimly lit room, most of which was lit with small red lights on computer consoles and the undersides of desks and tables, Amanda followed the road and soon would be able to place her Reaper into a loitering pattern above the intersection of Route 42 and Route 6 North…and wait.

2: 34 a.m., Wednesday, Syria

Amanda Johnson had been following the group of four vehicles, all alone on the road early in the pre-dawn hours in Syria. She had hoped the small convoy would lead her to other possible targets for the Reaper.

Below, the trucks' headlights made them easy to see, although the Reaper's sophisticated radar array, including infrared, didn't require the lights in order for Amanda to see them clearly on her display. The drone's cameras allowed her to see details as small as the fluttering of the canvas covering the cargo in Omar's truck bed.

U.S. intelligence sources had indicated that here, in this western part of Syria, Syrian air defenses were non-existent. It was the perfect place for what Amanda would do next.

Now, after more than five hours on the road, Omar saw the sign for Resafa and turned left onto Route 6. Two other trucks had just done so, and one was closing in on his truck to make the turn next.

4:37 p.m., Wednesday, Nevada, USA

Amanda Johnson lined up the first of the four trucks in the Reaper's camera sight. Normally, a Reaper pilot handled the controls and another operator handled the sensors. Her group was experimenting with a new console that allowed the pilot to take over both functions.

This was the first time Amanda would be trying it, but it didn't look any more difficult than a video game. She had seen it done many times and had done dozens of mock flights to prepare. She was ready.

2:37 a.m., Thursday, Syria

The truck was moving at about 40 miles per hour now. She could see it clearly with the drone's thermal sight. She steadied her grip and pushed the button that with less than a two-second delay, facilitated by a satellite link, would release the first of the drone's Hellfire II missiles. She then lined up the shot on the second truck and fired. Two large explosions flooded the thermal sight with brilliant flashes of light. Secondary explosions were visible from the largest of the trucks, which Amanda surmised had contained mostly explosives.

Omar stepped on the brakes. The vehicle behind him continued to get closer. Omar worried that the truck might hit his, until a massive flash of light and a deafening explosion behind him obliterated it. One Hellfire missile remained.

The last missile was for Omar's truck. There was no time to pray to Allah when it struck. Omar Ahmad, ISIS driver and Amanda Johnson, C.I.A. operator, had met for one brief instant in time. Their destinies had merged at the intersection of Route 42 and Route 6 in this remote part of Syria. This convoy of pharmaceuticals and ammunition would not make it to Ar Raqqah, nor to Abu Kama in Iraq. There would be no more Keflex for Aakil Farid.

Amanda wasn't convinced that Omar and the other drivers would go to paradise and be greeted by the promised 72 virgins. For her part, she got up from the console, stretched, and got another Diet Coke.

C H A P T E R

Epilogue

Mike arose early on Saturday morning. He didn't have to go in to the office today, but he did have plans to go see an important client. He showered and shaved, and after a quick breakfast, gathered some things and put them in the black, leather portfolio he used to keep his documents in as he traveled to meet with his policy holders.

He walked to the parking garage that was Ghost's home and the old Mercedes jumped to life as he turned the key in the ignition. Easing out onto Richmond's maze of one-way streets, he soon merged onto I-95 North and then onto I-64 East, then over to Richmond-Henrico Turnpike.

Parking along the narrow roadway, he walked the short distance. He remembered the location. Holy Cross Cemetery was Marv's final resting place. At the grave, he paused, placed a U.S. Marine Corps challenge coin on top of the headstone, and bowed his head in prayer.

"Marv, I hope you'll accept this Marine Corps honor, even though you were Army. Nobody's perfect!" He smiled as the thought ran silently through his mind. Here, inter-service rivalry meant nothing except as a token of respect and affection between two men who had served their country.

"Because of you, and with the help of Cathy and a lot of other people, we got the greedy bastards responsible for your death and probably the deaths of hundreds or maybe even thousands of other veterans and their family members."

"I'm so sorry it took losing you to make that happen, but you didn't die in vain. Because of you, nobody else will be dying from the counterfeit drugs going to the military. May God bless you and reward you for your service and for the good life you lived. I hope to see you again sometime. Save me a cold beer up there!"

He reached into the portfolio and removed the laminated front-page of the Richmond Times-Dispatch with the bold headline, "**U.S. Senator, Others Arrested in Counterfeit Prescription Drug Case.**" The lead article detailed the events leading up to Senator Royce's arrest and contained this sentence, "My good friend Marvin Kincaid died needlessly because Senator Royce and others in this country and Mexico were greedy. I hope these arrests allow Marv to rest in peace knowing that justice will be served,' said Michael DePalma, a local insurance agent who had Kincaid as a client."

Mike leaned the page against the headstone, saluted slowly, then turned and walked back to his car. He wondered if the F.B.I. and Mexican authorities truly had gotten everyone involved.

The former administration had bungled a lot of things--like providing guns to Mexican drug cartels. The numerous scandals that occurred during those eight years were still coming to light even now. He wondered for a minute if even the ex-president or his vice president could have had any role in this whole counterfeiting operation and its infiltration into the nation's military pharmacy system—especially since they were both quite anti-military.

For that moment, he wondered...if a senator could be involved, why not someone else? He dismissed the thought.

Damn, he was going to miss Marv.

But now, it was time to head home to pack for Chicago.

As he walked from Marv's grave toward Ghost, a drop of morning dew seemed to run down his cheek.

Marines don't cry," he thought.

— E N D —

About the Author

Don J. Kappel is a retired U.S. Marine Corps major and former adjunct professor who has taught English Composition at Coastal Carolina Community College in Jacksonville, North Carolina and Journalism at Temple University in Philadelphia. His military career took him to Japan, Cuba, South Korea, the Philippines, Iraq and many duty stations in the U.S., including Headquarters, U.S. Marine Corps, where he served as head of the Community Relations branch of the Public Affairs Division and later as an official U.S. Marine Corps spokesman in the Media branch.

His articles have been published in numerous military; local government; professional and commercial publications. He also has served as a media consultant and has conducted public relations and media relations seminars and webinars for U.S. and international audiences.

Made in the USA
Columbia, SC
11 March 2020

88848635R00130